THE COMMONPLACE DAY

Elizabeth Westbury, mother of two, has been married to Tim for seventeen years. With her comfortable domestic life and a circle of friends in suburban London, she has all the trappings of a contented existence. However, she has a vague but distressing feeling that life is passing her by. Unable to pinpoint exactly what she is looking for, she craves an escape from the tedious demands of day-to-day tasks. Her dissatisfaction focuses on Dobie, an old friend, and she convinces herself that an affair with him would give meaning to her pointless existence.

THE COMMONPLACE DAY

The Commonplace Day

by

Rosemary Friedman

Dales Large Print Books
Long Preston, North Yorkshire,
BD23 4ND, England.

British Library Cataloguing in Publication Data.

Friedman, Rosemary
    The commonplace day.

    A catalogue record of this book is
    available from the British Library

    ISBN   978-1-84262-745-7 pbk

Dales Large Print is an imprint of Library Magna Books Ltd.

Printed and bound in Great Britain by
T.J. (International) Ltd., Cornwall, PL28 8RW

For

PRISCILLA,

with love

No day is commonplace if we had only eyes to see its splendour.

EMERSON

Life consists in what man is thinking of all day.

EMERSON

PART ONE

One

I woke at seven and thought stewing steak and ring about the cooker then turned over and went to sleep again. The next thing I knew was the slight click of saucer on glass, my cup of tea, and Tim saying come on it's half-past and feeling sorry for myself having to get up as though I hadn't had a wink of sleep, although in fact I'd been out for the count since quarter to eleven.

It was always the same, the feeling of resentment and that if left in peace I would sleep contentedly until doomsday; except on Sundays when I didn't have to get up, no school or anything, and Tim prepared his own breakfast, and I'd be awake at seven bright as a button and raring to go, nowhere.

Foggy, he said, pulling the curtains back but I knew because it had drifted into the room and the back of my throat was lumpy from breathing it in all night. It wasn't cold because ignoring the fuel merchant's plea to 'buy a bigger bunker', we'd had central-heating installed, unable to let the rest of the 'village' bang and clank and heave out their soot-ridden boilers without us. The new boiler came on automatically at 6.30 and shunted merrily in its little garden house until with a sudden shudder it would stop and into the quiet Tim would say, It's vibrating, needs cleaning, must ring old Jellaby; he'd done the whole road and we were his family, his children, but of course the day would go by and neither of us would do anything about it.

The tea was a joke really because Tim came from a tea-drinking family and I did not. I'd been married for seventeen years and still disliked making tea for my in-laws. It was either too weak or too strong or too thin, not enough body, or you hadn't shaken the milk bottle properly, or there was, horror of horrors, a leaf, I could never find the strainer; and even if the brew was right, which was rare, there was the question of temperature. It had to be hot but not too hot. There were so many permutations that it was almost impossible to hit on just the correct formula for the *Légion d'honneur* of the tea-drinkers' union the acclaim of the 'nice cup'. I never began to understand, probably I did not want to; that was why Tim always made his own.

The joke part came in with my cup which Tim set religiously on the bedside table each morning at 7.30. If I was indifferent to tea during the day, before breakfast I actively loathed the stuff. I always heaved myself up and took one sip, like medicine, and flopped back on to the pillow, exhausted, waiting for the stimulant effect I firmly believed it to possess. Sometimes I tried to multiply seventeen by the number of days in a year, less fifty-two Sundays, in an attempt to work out how many gallons or bathfuls or reservoirs of tea I had poured down the sink since we'd been married. It always became too involved and I got lost, like with Robin's homework when the men and the shovels and the earth they had to remove in the requisite number of days became confused, and I gave up.

Tim had the newspaper under his arm and went into the bathroom and I heard him turn on the water. I always waited for the sound of it before I relinquished the last vestige of semi-consciousness and unwillingly I arose, like Venus from the foam, and took my sip.

I allowed myself five minutes, aware that it was a luxury. Some women were up at six or even 5.30 with a day's work done before I opened my eyes. Perhaps they didn't think, I told myself, when, after all, did they have time? Up for the household chores, out to work, back for more chores, no energy remaining except perhaps for telly and bed. Probably it was just as well, not thinking I mean, although I knew it was the what-might-have-been fantasies, indulged in in these moments of quiet, that kept me sane. Sane. Well enough of sanity remaining to have managed to date without the pills and visits to the analyst upon which Martha was now quite dependent, and without the shock therapy which was no longer a remote mystique belonging to psychiatry but something that actually happened to people one knew. True there were the small blue capsules, the thin edge, I often imagined, of the wedge. I was unable to sleep without them but on most nights I did not need to take them. This paradox was due to the fact that although I only took them when I knew that the following day was to bring some particular stress I felt unable to cope with unaided, I had to know that they were there, available if necessary. The comforting sight of the smoky brown bottle next to the bed would ensure a good night's sleep secure in the knowledge that if the teeming brain refused to close down for the night the remedy was at hand. It sounds terribly neurotic. Heather who went to keep-fit with all those sweaty women, shopped at the Health Food Stores, and said they mixed antibiotics with the cattle-cake and all our food was contaminated, said that it was. Tim said Heather was just as neurotic, unable to live without her daily-dozen and wheat germ and all that, and that there was

16

nothing to choose between us.

I was a pillow reformer. I never got between the cold sheets at night, Tim wouldn't have an electric blanket, without reminding myself of those lacking one blanket, let alone four and a quilted Terylene eiderdown, and dwelt often upon the plight of the pot-bellied, stick-armed waifs who looked appealingly out from the Oxfam advertisements. We sent parcels, of course, all of us in the 'village' did, Robin and Diana's cast-offs, and raised money in our various ways. We never really 'did' anything though; not like it used to be. The Spanish Civil War for instance when people actually went to fight or be nurses, or even our own war when older sisters nonchalantly drove ambulances, undeterred by falling bombs. Things had changed. You raised money and sent your old shirt when it was no longer any use to you. You read the papers and clucked with sympathy but you never physically responded to causes. Our lot did not, at any rate. There were those, of course, plenty of them, who in an excess of King Canute-ism were willing to march under tolerably difficult conditions and to sit down in defiance of the law in a misguided attempt to stem the tide of the nuclear era. Always, though, they cohered in nice cosy little hundreds where nothing more terrible than a fine or a few uncomfortable nights in prison was likely to occur, and those in good,

17

worthy company. Possibly it was a naïve concept to imagine that the only helping hand was the one which literally filled the empty bowl in some remote corner of the earth. The money had, after all, to be raised, the organisation administered, which would send the man, pay for the food, which went into the bowl. A great many cogs were necessary but were there not too many, myself among them, standing impotently in the midst of paperweights whose walls were not glass, but the comforts and good living to which we had gradually become conditioned? The thousand and one aids to existence swirled round us like snow and outside this cosmos of our own creating survival was impossible. I pictured the ultimate cataclysm as the final smashing, atomically if you like, of the millions of these insulated paperweights from which those who did not succumb would crawl slowly, naked, innocent as they were born, to do what they would with their second chances. This again was probably ingenuous. We never would live in a world fit for heroes, nor fight the war to end all wars. These were clichés coined for the benefit of the mutilated and the bereaved, and had little to do with reality which would mutilate and bereave as long as it chose.

'It's twenty-five to,' Tim said, 'and Diana can't find her stockings.' He looked with resignation at the cup. 'You haven't drunk your tea.'

He said it every morning. It really was time to leave the impossible state the world had got itself into and deal with the minor universe in which I could do some tiny good even if it was only to find Diana's stockings.

They were in the airing cupboard as I'd thought they would be. She hadn't troubled to move anything and they were hidden by her swimming towel.

She was sitting in bed in her vest, beneath the vacuous faces of the latest pop group, reading.

'You didn't look.'

She jabbed a finger on the page. 'I did. Where were they?'

'If you'd taken the trouble to move something...' It was an old record and I sensed her ears automatically closing, saw her eyes slide back to the book. She'd surrounded herself with shirt, tunic, tie, knickers, everything even to her cardigan and slunk back to bed. I was about to make the speech concerning open windows and stripped beds and brisk dressing but the very thought of it made me shudder, anyway it was foggy, so I just said, 'Hurry, you'll be late,' and left her to it.

It was cold in the kitchen. Lower temperature humph humph, Mr Jellaby said, heat of the cooker supplements the rad; but the cooker wasn't cooking first thing in the morning and it was always bleak. There were puddles of tea left by Tim on the canary yellow Formica tops, an empty bottle of gin put out last night after Martha and Jack, the bird's nest of brown paper straw from a chocolate box, yesterday's newspapers.

I let up the grey venetian blinds, mopped up the tea with a clammy Wettex, and switched the hot-plate on for the porridge. The table in the dinette with its trailing-ivy wallpaper was already set. I always did what I could the night before being at my absolute worst in the mornings. I could hardly blame Diana. There was really something in it. I'd read it in the *Reader's Digest*. Something to do with body temperatures and how some people's was at its lowest in the mornings. They were almost in a state of hibernation. It summed me up exactly.

The cooker was new, or had been almost a year ago when it was delivered with a chip in the enamel top. We complained to the retailer who said he would contact the manufacturer and see that a new top was delivered right away. Right away. Weeks rolled by, then it was Christmas, Madam, and the factory closed. After that they really were sending someone to inspect the damage and replace the part but they had trouble with the vans, maintenance or something, then the particular top for our model was out of stock for the moment, then the summer holidays intervened. They were closed once more, then we were away. I forgot to chase them up when we returned and now, fantastic as it appeared, it was getting round to Christmas again. I put the saucepan on the hotplate. I had grown used to the chip. I was fed up with telephoning, waiting for the right man in the right department, hardly cared now if they brought a new top or not; it was not after all a very big chip. Tim insisted though, the thing was new, had been at any rate, and you couldn't accept shoddy stuff it was expensive enough. It was shoddy too; the inside of the oven was almost impossible to clean the finish was so poor. I remembered my mother's cooker, an enormous old thing, grey, not white and shiny like ours. She'd had it for years and years and years and the surface was impeccable, diamond hard, and only needed a wipe. It was the same with the refrigerator constructed of fiddly plastic compartments saying 'butter' and 'cheese', only after the first few weeks you didn't bother, which snapped at the slightest provocation. Similarly with everything. The American idea really, we were becoming more and more like the Americans. Everything had to be changed every five minutes for new models, nothing was made to endure. You were constantly in a stage of replacing something, aided in your choice by the glossy ads, in accordance with the theory of obsolescence.

I felt something hard and painful in the small of my back.

'Go and sit down, Robin, breakfast is almost ready.'

He put the revolver on the fridge, not gently, another scratch.

'Have the papers come?'

'I suppose so.'

'Where are they?'

'Upstairs.'

'Did they send my comic?'

'Better ask Daddy. Not now. It's ready. You'll be late.'

'Won't be a mo.'

I put his bowl on the table. 'Tell Diana to hurry.'

Diana had bought me a gadget called a 'Forget-me-not' for my birthday. It was made of red plastic and hung on the wall with green pegs which you manoeuvred to point to the item of shopping you required. It was a composite list beginning with bacon, and ending, through disinfectant and puddings, with vegs. The only trouble was that either I never remembered to put the appropriate peg down or Robin, unwittingly or deliberately, manipulated them in all directions indicating that we were in need of bleach or sausages when we were nothing of the kind.

Ignoring this *aide-memoire* I wrote stewing steak, veg, pots, on the back of one of Tim's letters and looking in the vegetable cupboard added mush, toms and, as a gallant afterthought at the trouble I was going to, flaky pastry. I ought really to order something for tomorrow while I was at it but couldn't think, wishing as usual that they'd invent some new kind of food. There were different recipes, of course, and cuts, and in my chi-chi moods which came every so often, I went specially to Harrods or Soho for sprigs of rosemary or blades of mace. Once I even bought a pestle and mortar, which we used now as an ashtray in the bathroom, because I saw a picture of the Hon. Mrs Somebody or other in her herby Knightsbridge kitchen, knocking up a little dinner party for ten in her best dress and pearls, and saying you simply couldn't get the authentic flavour unless you pestle-and-mortared it yourself. On that particular occasion Tim said what on earth have you done to the beef and, my God you didn't open the '57 Burgundy, anything but the '57, I was keeping that for old Bland, you know how he is about wines. There had been other phases; trout with almonds and tiny little vol-au-vents. It was a particularly cold night and Tim said, No soup? And in spite of myself I delivered a speech about trying to make you something different, to

23

add a little variety, and he said it's very good I only asked if there was any soup. I said it's taken me all the afternoon and you don't even *care,* all you want is soup. I merely *asked* if there was soup. I don't know what you're getting excited about. I'm not getting excited. Tears and recriminations then, mostly because I'd let the vol-au-vent mixture catch when Martha phoned and I knew you could taste it.

Robin spread his comic over Tim's place and started on his porridge.

'Did you tell Diana?'

'What?'

'To hurry.'

'Didn't tell me to.'

'I did. You never listen. Take your elbows off.'

'Diana!'

'What are you screaming for?' Tim leaned over the banisters in his bathrobe.

'Tell Diana breakfast is getting cold.'

'Have you seen my cuff-links?'

'I may have put them in the laundry box. You have others.'

'I don't like the others. I wish you wouldn't.'

'Sorry. Tell Diana.'

She came down without washing her face.

'Do you like my hair like this?'

It drooped like a curtain on both sides with no parting, flicking up at the ends. At eighteen it would have been stunning, at twelve she looked a minx.

'I'd be more impressed if you'd washed.'

'I did!'

'What with?' Robin said.

'Mind your own business.'

He didn't lift his head from his comic. 'It couldn't have been soap because I took it for my experiment.'

'Molly Valentine's bought her parents a house,' Diana said. 'She's Top of the Pops.'

I thought I'd recognised the hairstyle.

'We get our Science back today.'

I made the coffee. 'The one Daddy tested you on?'

'Yes. He got my profit and loss wrong on Friday. He said put it on top and you're supposed to put it underneath.'

'If you did it yourself you'd have nothing to grumble about. You aren't supposed to have help.'

'I couldn't do them.'

'You must have had it explained.'

'She goes over it too quickly.'

'Surely you can ask if you don't understand.'

She gave me a withering look from beneath the hair. 'I'd look a proper nit.'

'It's better to look a "nit" surely...'

It was not. Since my day the old order had changed. Everything had changed; for better or worse I don't know but there were few points of similarity. At school we had been a mixed bunch taking life casually, not battling with gritted teeth against top people as Diana had to in the school we'd been lucky to get her into. In my class there had been Kate, I remember, whose father was a film director, who got the most appalling marks, Joyce who never managed to master even simple equations, but painted like an angel. June who was a superb mimic and kept us and the staff in stitches, Hazel who won us every netball match with her shooting, and Pam who never could get her tongue round the French verbs no matter how much Mamselle shouted. There were a few 'dead keens'. Barbara, with her thick glasses devoid of humour, Anne whose parents were physicists, Jean dead set on biochemistry. We worked, of course, at times we had to, but life was not so intense; not like it was for Diana who had been brainwashed with ideas of her own importance at getting into the school and instilled with an urgent need to fight her way to the top. She took too little time to laugh, to sing, to play; how could she with the ultimate disgrace, like the sword of Damocles, constantly over her head, the fear of being made to look a 'nit'.

Tim came down the stairs like a herd of elephants, looking vulnerable in his very white shirt and city suit, and smelling of the after-shave lotion Diana had bought for his birthday. He put a slice of bread into the toaster, removed Robin's comic from his place at the table, and sat down, unfolding the newspaper. I felt sorry for him.

They were my family, the fruits of my seventeen-year-old marriage, and I scrambled eggs for them while they passed each other the butter and the sugar and the marmalade and made desultory breakfast noises.

Robin was finished first and went upstairs, his nose still in the comic, then Diana when she'd got money for savings and Miss Harrison's present, Miss Harrison was leaving to get married, out of Tim.

Tim and I wondered between us whether there would shortly be a General Election, I tried to care, and I promised him I really would get on to them again about the cooker. He finished his second cup of coffee and I called to the children not to keep him waiting. He kissed me, hugging me to him a little, with an arm round my shoulder, and went to get the car out. I called upstairs again and Robin came down sounding just like Tim and gave me a wet smacking kiss, and had the belt of his raincoat twisted about three times. Diana inclined her head, a formality, not really touching my face, and she still didn't smell of soap, but I couldn't be bothered to argue, Tim was hooting. She picked up her leather bag, only nits wore satchels, which weighed about a ton, and was off in her beige stretch nylons. The door slammed, shaking the whole house, Robin. Suddenly it was quiet and they were gone.

I sat down at the wreckage of the breakfast table and poured coffee in the silence into the one clean cup and allowed the thought to creep out, for there was no-one but myself to hear it, that this was the day on which for the first time I was going to be unfaithful to my husband.

Two

It was very quiet in the kitchen after all of them. The tap was dripping. Tim always complained I never could turn a tap off properly, nor tune in a radio, nor stick down an envelope for that matter. Being an accountant he was very efficient in all these matters, having a tidy sort of brain. I enjoyed the coffee among the debris, Diana hadn't folded her napkin and had left crusts of toast. I was able to relax even under the forbidding eyes of what I called my butler and my footman; the dishwasher, without which life was unthinkable, and the fully automatic clothes-washer and dryer. We had installed them a year ago when we finally decided we could no longer give house room to the series of young ladies from the Continent who were misfits in their own homes and, in their coloured stockings and exotic hair-do's, came to disrupt ours. The decision which had been muzzily formulating during months of discontent over the rising telephone bill, and letters with foreign stamps provoking tears or days of sulks, which in turn led to scorched shirts and broken crockery, had been finally clinched as the result of what we called in the 'village' our scandal. There was scandal enough behind our respectable middle-class curtains, Terylene for the most part, with lace insertions, but this was something which touched us all. We had coffee on it for weeks afterwards. Even now it sprang back into my mind when I saw some luscious piece of Switzerland or Scandinavia disdainfully propelling a push-chair or hanging uninterestedly on to the reins of some tiny child in the High Street.

Reggie Stevens had always been one for the girls. At a party or even in the street he always had his hands all over you till Monica sighing said, Reggie, and like a schoolboy caught in the act he'd slink away somewhere where he thought she couldn't see him. Reggie and Monica gave houseroom to one Danielle who came from Paris and, as Tim said, really was an eyeful. When poor Monica came home early from town one day and found her in bed with Reggie it pulled us all up a bit sharply.

Half the 'village' sensibly enough were mechanised already. Those of us who were not installed every bit of mechanical aid we could wheedle out of our husbands and put ads in the local newspaper for Daily Helps who wanted, and got, five shillings an hour. They did have their own husbands though and were not addicted in the summer-time to walking round the house in bikinis. My own ad produced Mrs MacSweeney who should in precisely two minutes, the electric wall clock said two minutes to nine, push open the back door. Clasping the milk bottles and Robin's yoghurt, which she had collected from the back step, to her bosom she would reply to my greeting of 'good morning' with the sad comment that it was not a very nice one. After the scandal we all wondered what was going to happen to Monica and Reggie now that he had actually been caught in *flagrant delicto* with Danielle. None of us imagined for a moment that at number eleven, Monica and Reggie's house, distinguished by the flagpole on the front lawn, the *ménage à trios* would continue. That was what did, to the absolute astonishment of us all, happen. While the rest of us slowly but surely, and often with un-Christian glee, got rid of our Gerdas and Helgas and Hildegardes, Monica and Reggie continued to have their tea brought to them in bed every morning by the now repentant Danielle. It was a situation none of us pretended to understand, but one on which we felt we couldn't question Monica too deeply. Iris Sayers said Monica had muttered something about not wanting to admit defeat but we could not see how she could endure the sight of the girl in the house, let alone be pleasant to her and give her pocket

31

money every week.

The side gate opened then clicked into place again as Mrs MacSweeney closed it tidily after her. I quickly finished the rest of my coffee, not liking to be stood over while I breakfasted.

'Good morning, Mrs Mac.' My smile did not come easily first thing. I made an attempt, knowing it was neither first thing nor even second for her. Her husband left the house at six with a packed lunch.

'Not a very nice one.' She clutched the bottles with the furry gloves I had given her for Christmas.

'Foggy isn't it?'

'Clearing a bit now.' She coughed in an exaggerated manner. 'Gets right down your throat.'

'Put the kettle on and make a cup of tea.'

Only her eyes lit up. She never said thank you for anything.

'Goes right through you.' She put the milk bottles down on the draining board and, following her daily ritual, pulled off a glove, took a handkerchief from the pocket of her coat which was trimmed with imitation Persian lamb, and blew her nose, making it red.

I started to clear the breakfast because I wanted her to turn out the bathrooms.

She said: 'I'll do that,' untying the satin ribbon inside her coat.

'I thought you might give the bathrooms a good do today.'

Tim said why don't you just *tell* her. You are employing her. He didn't understand the species, who came to oblige, not work, and took umbrage and left if one suggested by word or deed they did not know their own jobs.

'I was thinking they needed a do,' Mrs Mac said thus saving her face, and hanging her coat in the cupboard from whence she extracted her overall.

The next step was more tricky.

'The Hoover seems to be rather full.' I occupied myself with the removal of crumbs from the toaster.

For a moment I thought she hadn't heard and I should have to humiliate myself once more. She was threading the tie of her overall through the slot. She wrapped it round her skinny waist and made a firm bow.

'My one's got paper bags,' she said taking her hat off. ''Course it's a later model than what yours is.'

I ceded the point not wishing to explain, in my defence, that after the dishwasher and the new Bendix Tim had put his foot down over the Hoover. He said, and he was probably right, that the old ones Hooved as well as the new and pointed out that his mother had had hers for twenty-seven years.

Mrs Mac patted her hair into shape. 'The

dust flies all over,' she said, 'when you empty it. I've been having trouble with my sinuses.'

I pictured her at the doctor's blaming the antiquated apparatus with which she had to work for the inflamed condition of her membranes.

It wasn't only the Hoover. She had taken pains over the months to make me aware that her spin-dryer spun faster, her television loomed larger, and her equipment in general was in every way superior to mine. True she didn't boast a demon which ground noisily to powder everything fed to it down the sink. Her Ted, she said, considered them dangerous, and that was that. Apart from this, according to Mrs Mac, the gadgets in number eight Laurel Gardens, the neat semi to which we delivered her on inclement mornings, or when there was a bus strike, were in every way superior to our own. There was one minor difference. Ours were paid for. Hers were not.

Having changed her shoes, putting her outdoor ones neatly into the cupboard beside the carpet sweeper, Mrs Mac pulled on her yellow rubber gloves, she suffered from dermatitis, also my fault, and started to wipe the milk bottles. There was one further step in our parley before I could escape upstairs.

'How is Ted?' I said. 'And the children?'

She was putting the bottles in the fridge.

Hers defrosted automatically.

'Ted's all right,' she said. Ted was in light industry and always making trouble with the Union, with complaints about the sanitary arrangements and such-like. 'Chrissie's still chesty. I've been rubbing her in with Vapoid.'

I thought of the Vapoid advertisement on television. A saccharine little girl, with missing front teeth and a frilly nighty, clutched a huge teddy bear, while an even more saccharine mother sniffed the Vapoid jar as though it was marijuana, to the accompaniment of saccharine music. To Mrs MacSweeney it was not in the slightest oversweet. The plump child in the studio had become confused in her mind with the puny, unprepossessing Chrissie, and the smiling mother, who wanted to do the best for her child, undistinguishable from herself. The result of all this was a visit to the chemist and Vapoid. By the same process she spent a large proportion of her wages on peas, 'sweeter than the day they were picked', sausages, which were 'chopped, never minced', and cat food made of revolting little whole fishes incarcerated in jelly.

'This fog doesn't help,' she said, looking out of the window at the garden shrouded in mist. 'Weather gets worse and worse. I'll take her down the doctor's Saturday if she's still bad.'

She filled the kettle, to the top, indifferent to my electricity bills.

I put the last of the plates into the dish-washer and shut it.

'Shall I bring you a cup?' Mrs Mac said, plugging the kettle in.

'No thank you. I'm going to have my bath.'

I left her to it aware that before I reached the first stair the cigarettes and matches would be out of her overall pocket.

In the children's rooms there was mild chaos; in Diana's rather, because in Robin's room the mess was organised so I suppose you couldn't really call it chaos.

Watched by the petrified stares of the pop group I picked up three playing cards, a sus-pender belt, to which was attached one stocking, a Crunchie paper, and *Great Expectations*. On the wash-basin the flannel was bone dry although for a change the toothbrush was wet. She had probably run it under the tap. The room was pink with pink-and-white striped wallpaper on the wall behind the bed. We had had it redecorated for Diana's birthday and allowed her to choose the colour and the paper which was a mistake. She'd been thrilled to bits at the time and dragged everyone up to see it, even the fish boy. The pink was too pink and the stripe on the wallpaper far too heavy. Now she voted the whole thing revolting and said it was our fault for allowing her to choose. She had nagged about it for months. Sally had chosen her wallpaper and Cynthia who, if we were to believe all Diana told us, lived in a cross between the Negresco at Nice and Buckingham Palace, had herself picked everything for her room from Maples, even down to the Dresden toothbrush holder, which I thought was going a bit far. They were their own small worst enemies as we had recently begun to discover. Tim and I had started off as modern parents determined that our children should not suffer, as we had, the ignominy of no-one listening to our opinions, the dislike of being treated as small children far into adolescence, the shame of being seen and not heard. The mistake we made was to swing the pendulum too far and give the children a freedom they wanted but did not want; they begged for but were not equipped to cope with. With Diana, as in the case of the bedroom wallpaper, we found ourselves in the bewildering position of having our kindness flung back into our faces. It had been the same with the piano. Could she learn to play the piano? Everyone learned to play the piano. She adored the piano. She wanted to be a pianist. As a family we were strictly non-musical. Robin, of us all, was the only one able to sing a note and he was quite happy with the recorder he had made at school. We left it for a year thinking that it would blow over. For twelve months we seemed to hear nothing but piano, piano, piano, until we were under the impression that we were cruelly frustrating an incipient genius and began to scan the columns of the local newspaper for news of a secondhand piano. We tracked one down and installed it in the dining-room, where it spoiled the décor, and by the same medium a Miss Morani, who looked about a hundred and smelled of mothballs, but came highly recommended. All this was two years ago. We waited for our genius to emerge but nothing happened. Nothing that was except a trickle of uninspiring pieces, less inspiringly played, rushed in the easy bits, and extorted with agony in the more difficult. The piano became an object of hatred; Miss Morani likewise. Why did we ever make her learn the piano? We who had suffered. She never wanted to learn the piano in the first place. Couldn't she stop her piano lessons? But you nagged, Diana, you nagged and nagged, it was the thing you most wanted to do in the world. The world had changed. Did I?– Was she that innocent? – If I did I don't remember. I suppose two years out of twelve is quite a high proportion. In any case I don't want to learn any more. We were cruel parents. Fancy forcing anyone to learn the play the piano when they didn't want to learn to play the piano. We might have known,

Diana said, she wasn't musical. None of us were. It was then we discovered that they were more on our side than on their own, to which by tradition they were bound to adhere. We were not greatly surprised therefore when Diana told us that in the school debate she had opposed the motion that children should be allowed to watch television as much as they wished. Diana who branded us inquisitors nightly. Lately we had stuck to our guns impervious to impassioned accounts of the liberties and dispensations permitted, if we were to believe all we were told, which I no longer thought Diana really expected us to, by the parents of Cynthia and Sally and 'all the other people in my class'. Well, when questioned closely, 'nearly all'.

Robin was easier. His room too. There was not a great deal one was allowed to tidy. I folded his pyjamas which were in a heap on the floor, stepped across the railway lines which criss-crossed the carpet, leaned over the complicated cardboard calendar which told not only the day and the month, but the year and the weather and the temperature on the roof of thirty-four Hazelbank which was our house, and opened the window. With Robin we had none of the fluctuations of mood we suffered with Diana, but something which was in a way even more difficult to cope with; his bull-like obstinacy. Once Robin dug his heels in over anything it was, as with Tim's father, impossible to move him. We had to be one jump ahead all the time so that he did not find himself in a position from which he was incapable of capitulation. Like a permanent object lesson the Tower of London stuck firmly in our minds. The outing had been planned for weeks and the children were looking forward to it, Robin particularly. It was Saturday morning and Tim was playing golf. Diana run up and get ready I said, and Robin change your trousers, then we can have lunch and leave as soon as Daddy comes in. Robin was reading on the floor, a comic I suppose, he was always reading comics. He was eight at the time. These trousers are all right, he said, his nose still in the comic. You could see your face in the back of them. Don't be silly, go up and change, your others are on the bed. I'm not changing my trousers, no-one will see. You aren't going out like that. Why not? Because I said so. Go along now. Be a good boy. I'm not going; it's silly changing just for the Tower of London; I'll be wearing my mac anyway. Robin! I was getting angry. Go up and change and be quick about it. No. If you don't change your trousers you aren't going to the Tower. You can stay at home. We were wiser now. I'll stay at home then. Don't be silly; be a good boy now; wash and change. I'll wash but I'm not changing my trousers; these trousers are all right. You'll stay at home then. And he did. I don't know who had the more miserable afternoon; Diana and Tim and I gazing vacantly at the Crown Jewels with the knowledge of poor Robin at home spoiling our pleasure, or Robin himself defiantly reading the same comic over and over in the company of Suki from Finland who couldn't speak a word of English. We were careful now not to let these situations develop and were becoming masters of diplomacy at dealing with Robin. As long as we were able to avoid pitting our wills against his Robin was a lamb, no trouble at all. He belonged to Tim's family, and nowhere in him did I recognise myself.

In my own room there was only my mess. Tim was as tidy as his ordered mind dictated and there wasn't a thing of his about. I stripped the bed, ran the bath in the bathroom that opened off the bedroom, and wondered what I should wear in which to commit adultery.

The telephone rang and it was Martha so I could keep my thoughts, my real thoughts, for a little longer in the cage in which they were confined. I settled down on the bed for a while to prove an ear for the unorganised outpourings of Martha's cluttered mind.

The telephone was grey, one of the new, lightweight ones with a twisted plastic cord, and I lay down full length in my nylon dressing-gown and listened to the torrent of words which fell higgledy-piggledy out of the receiver.

We'd seen them only nine hours ago, the end of the gin reminding Jack that it was time to go, but Martha wanted to know how was I darling, not really listening to the answer, but telling me how she hadn't slept and had to get up at three o'clock and take a tablet. Now she felt as if a steam-roller had been over her. She had taken something or other 'zine to carry her through until her next session with her analyst and was hoping to God it would hurry up and work. I hung on while she found an ashtray then she started on the lounge curtains.

Martha and Jack were in the van of the suburban house renovators. Because of the recent inflationary rise in the price of property, moving, for most of us, was beyond our means. Jack had been doing extraordinarily well recently in property but not sufficiently well to make the transition to a town house which Martha would have liked. Instead, after the central heating and the terrace, which had become a *sine qua non* of 'village' life, they had converted their garage into a rumpus-room, American style, added a new double garage, above which was another bedroom and bathroom, and were now involved in a complete reconstruction of the ground floor.

They had started off with a fashionable interior decorator who said out with the staircase and a couple of walls. They took his advice then Martha had a row with him over the windows, he insisted on what Martha called fish-tank and hated, and he went off in a huff. They were now in the midst of a law-suit over his fees.

Michael, the pink-shirted youth who had replaced him, closed his gorgeous eyes despairingly, said they had removed quite the wrong walls and how sad they had not called him in the first place.

About the curtains Martha said on the other end of the telephone, what did I think of straw? They had decided on straw-coloured hessian for the walls and Michael said definitely the same for the curtains to preserve the unity.

It sounded deadly to me, all that straw-colouring, but Martha didn't really want my opinion just to air hers. Without waiting for an answer she started on under-floor heating, or did I think hot air ducts, and I suddenly remembered my bath. I'll speak to you later then, Martha said; how about lunch? I had to have lunch somewhere so I said all right, then was sorry because it might be difficult to get away. Martha said one o'clock at Bendick's and I hung up.

It was nearly up to the waste-pipe and the bathroom filled with steam. I put on the shower cap and some nourishing cream on my face taking it right down my neck, today was important, and got in.

The water slopped over the drain and I heard it gurgling down and thought Mrs Mac would be running up soon to say there's water coming from somewhere. For the moment though it was quiet and the water beautifully hot and I lay back until I was quite immersed except for my head and allowed myself to think about Dobbie.

Three

I wondered what he was doing. Had he stayed in all morning putting the tiger-skin rugs down on the floor, or had he gone to his office as usual? He had of course. For Dobbie it was an ordinary day, and I was probably down in his diary between lunch at the Savoy Grill and cocktails at the Polish Embassy, or one of the other Eastern European countries he did business with. He had interests in everything from cigars to citrus and travelled the world to administer them. Dobbie, of course, had nothing to lose. He was not going to pace the flat all day quaking in his shoes. Not that I was quaking. I had had long enough to make up my mind. There was no-one behind me pushing me into it, and I had been careful enough to be confident there were no sanctions ahead. I had lived through this particular day so many times in my dreams, both of the day and night variety, that I was not apprehensive as I might have been. Like an actress who had been through months of rehearsal I felt that I knew my part. There would probably be some first-night nerves but I was, if only through fantasy, familiar with my role. At any rate it would be better than car keys, a game played by a particular set in the village to which I did not belong.

It was Olga Tindal who had started it, and she'd brought it from America. It was horribly crude and I thought I was justified in thinking that it bore no relationship whatsoever to what I was contemplating with Dobbie.

Olga Tindal had been an absolute corker before she was married. She was one of those honey blondes about whom everything, when we were eighteen, was just right. She had an exquisite face with translucent green eyes, at which you just had to look twice, an enviable figure, and taut cream skin that begged for exposure in evening dresses or swim-suits. She had been amoral then, and I don't mean only as far as sex was concerned. She wove intricate lies, unable to differentiate in her own mind, I think, between fact and fantasy, spread the most appalling muck about people, and would let you down at the drop of a hairpin. She was the kind of girl who would date a nice, but not very interesting, boy for a night she happened to have free, and let him down, with no qualms whatsoever, if something more interesting turned up. It was the same with women. I'd always known Olga, our mothers were friends, and in spite of her characteristics, some of which were pretty foul, you could deny neither her beauty nor the charm that went with it. She was not to be relied on, though, for a moment. She was too busy feathering her own nest. She'd bought a fabulous dress, she'd say, and wanted to give it to you for five pounds because she'd put on weight and was unable to get into it. At five pounds it would seem a bargain. Then you'd sit down in it and discover that it creased so badly that it was unwearable. It was five pounds down the drain as Olga very well knew, although she'd open her green eyes innocently wide in denial. In the same way she would borrow your white satin evening bag and return it smudged with lipstick, books, and keep them, unimportant but annoying, and smaller things like Biros and hankies which you knew you could say goodbye to. The trouble with Olga was that you knew, and she knew too, that about her was an appealing quality, undefinable, which made it impossible to refuse her anything. Whether it was her eyes which she could almost liquefy at will or her smile, dazzling in those days, I don't know, but she had this mysterious quality of getting things from people and she had traded on it all her life. Out of all the boys who had revolved around her like moths around a flame, for some reason that none of us had ever been able to fathom, Olga had married Archie Tindal. Archie was a weedy little chap with a bottomless fund of filthy jokes and bedroom eyes. True he had money, but then so did a good many of the others who had courted Olga. Martha said that although Olga boasted that they did none of them ever asked her to marry him. After they'd slept with her, a pastime about which, in her own words, she wasn't fussy, they'd gone on to find somebody more discriminating. Whatever it was that promoted it she'd married Archie and had two daughters, one of whom looked fabulous like Olga and the other, poor little thing, like her father, although rumour had it she was clever. Not that Olga was any longer fabulous in appearance, although a lot of us would still give quite a bit for some of her looks even as she was now. She had ruined her honey-blonde hair with bleaches. Some weeks she was pink, some feathered gold and silver, some platinum. She wore it short now and very formal, exaggeratedly high or wide according to the fashion. It was not her hair though which had changed most. It was her face; that gorgeous, open face. There were no lines on it. Her skin still, in her thirties, was with no exaggeration like the finest porcelain. It was the expression which had altered. At eighteen it had betrayed the fact that she considered the world was hers; at thirty-six it showed that she was no longer sure but was engaged in a bitter fight to make it so. Her eyes which before were inviting, were calculating, her mouth which had been soft, mobile, twitched with dissatisfaction. You wouldn't think she had anything to be dissatisfied about. She had a lovely house and a bronze Renault Floride with an open top, and a black poodle and two nice children and, of all of us, a maid in a cap and apron. About Olga now there was a sort of desperateness as though she'd been under the impression that life had promised her something else; as if she'd been cheated and didn't know quite whom to blame. I think that all of us in the 'village' felt this way to a certain extent. There was about us a restlessness which was difficult to define. We were happy, most of us, prima facie at any rate, but we eyed each other with a kind of predatory wariness in case one of us achieved something the other hadn't. It was not simply a question of keeping up with the Joneses but something more subtle than a yearning for material things. This vague awareness, for it was no more than that, of something that had passed us by was perhaps best reflected in the way we read avidly in our newspapers of the nightly shenanigans of the notorious, the titled and the wealthy and felt ourselves, by comparison, to be living in a curious and unsettling limbo. We had good, hard-working husbands, children, two cars in the garage. We were happy; yet we were not. We had the impression, unvoiced but running like a nebulous common denominator through the 'village', that we had missed something. Like Olga we did not quite know what.

Olga had always entertained a great deal. She'd taken a course at the Cordon Bleu School and her parties, over which she went to a great deal of trouble, were always beautifully done. She had help with the preparation and the serving but she always did the cooking herself and the dishes she prepared, especially when it was a cold buffet, were an experience both to look at and to eat.

In the early days Tim and I had usually been invited. We were fairly friendly and the evenings at the Tindals' were always enjoyable, although inclined to be a bit much when Archie really got started on his jokes. After we'd all been married for a while though, and were shaking down in the 'village', we discovered that Olga and Archie were collecting about them a different crowd and that we didn't really fit in. Olga had always been a bit of a collector, of people that was, and she and Archie gradually built up around them a new set, and little by little dropped their old friends. We were still on good terms, talking about our children or old times when we met in the hairdresser's or the fishmonger's, but we were no longer on visiting terms except occasionally at Christmas or when they decided to have a cocktail party and include a bloc as it were from the old guard. The criteria for membership of Olga and Archie's new set were, I believe, money, the sort that came in lashings, small fame of some sort – periphery film and stage people – or notoriety in the sexual field. In addition to these they ferreted out the other Olgas and Archies of the 'village', those, that is, who were not averse to a change of partner now and again.

The idea of the car keys game was this. The Tindals or one of the other couples arranged a party. When the company was assembled and had been well dined and wined, the men threw their car keys into a hat where they were shaken and picked, one each, blindfold, by the women. The owner of the car key each picked was her sleeping partner for the night, or perhaps the evening. I don't know the details. It was as simple as that, and if one believed all reports, tremendous fun. According to Martha it had caught on like wild-fire in the suburbs of America and wasn't doing at all badly here.

I did not equate myself with Olga.

Neither did I have any illusions.

I have known Dobbie from childhood, but then I have known Tim that long too. They were at school with my brother Gray, who owed his name to the fact that Mother had a thing about Somerset Maugham at the time of his birth, although he and Dobbie were quite a bit older than Tim.

Perhaps my first real memory of Dobbie, as a person, not as a child, was when I was six, Dobbie and Gray thirteen. It was Gray's birthday. He had been given an enormous constructional kit, he loved building, and we were on the floor with it in his bedroom, which ran the length of the top of the house, and was already full of railways, vintage cars, and aeroplanes he had made. I remember Gray saying, I know, we'll build a complete village, houses, shops, church, that sort of thing, and getting quite excited. Dobbie got up and looked out of the window. His name was Arthur Dobson but he was Dobbie to everyone. I hate houses, he said. I hate building things; except skyscrapers. I like everything to be big and to move about all over the place.

It was badly expressed, perhaps, but it summed up exactly Dobbie's attitude to life. He hated things small and settled like Gray, who had become an architect, and now lived happily at Cookham in a house he had built himself.

Gray's house was modern and orderly like Gray himself, his wife Diana, and their daughter Jennifer who seemed never to bring mud into, or scatter her belongings about, the open plan. Everything slid or was concealed, and really was tremendously elegant with a whacking view of the river through the picture windows. I always had the impression, when visiting them, that I was waiting for something and had discovered one day that it was the salesman, who I felt sure was going to pop out, old school tie and rubbing his hands, from between the curved Heals' sofa, seven foot long, and the teak wall unit, Swedish, which housed drinks, a television set, and many of the other necessities of modern living, including books with shiny covers which I don't think any of them read much.

Gray always mixed the drinks himself and was fussy about them, wiping the glasses first with a coloured tea-towel printed with vodka bottles, kept especially for the purpose, and bringing your glass complete with coaster.

Dobbie had a flat in Knightsbridge, but the world was his High Street. He was equally at home in Rotterdam or Hong Kong, New York or Bulawayo. He liked everything to be big, he said, and took planes for San Francisco as easily as the bus for Selfridges. His view of the wood had never been obscured by the trees.

In those childhood days when he spoke of the things he was going to do and be I suppose he represented to me a world of adventure, a world where anything was likely to happen.

He still did.

When Tim and I were coping with measles, or a period of no domestic help, or frozen pipes, a postcard would arrive from Dobbie from somewhere on the far side of the world, conjuring up blue skies and tepid seas, and an existence far removed from our own.

Whenever he was in England he'd ring us up or sometimes not even bother, just walk in and stay for dinner, and spend the evening taking us out of our rut with accounts of things he had done and people he had met in various parts of the globe. He loved relaxing with us, he said, it made him see what he, a bachelor, was missing in the way of domestic bliss. We knew he didn't mean it. That it was all right for an evening or two, but after that the novelty would pall and he would be itching to be off. He loved the children, wasn't at all bored by them, again I suppose it was the novelty. Often he carted them off to the zoo and told them about the elephants he had seen in their natural surroundings, and to the circus and pantomime, people like Dobbie never seemed to have to book up, and to Claridges for lunch.

I'd often wondered what he would be like to sleep with. Any woman must have done. Dobbie was as handsome as Gregory Peck or Cary Grant or any of those clean-looking actors of the older school, not the mean-looking method boys of today. Just recently I'd noticed his jaw as losing its clear outline a little, and sometimes there were little pockets of puffy flesh beneath his eyes. These in no way detracted from the general picture of what was known as a man's man but was in reality every lady's man. He was over six foot and broad-shouldered and looked good in lounge suit, dinner jacket, or sweater; similarly he was equally at home in office, night club, or on skis of the snow or water variety. The only picture of him at which the imagination really baulked was the domestic one, doing dishes, gardening, walking a crying baby in the night. He did these things occasionally when he was with us but it was as if he was playing a part and not to the manner born. Whenever Dobbie came I always looked my best. I don't think that Tim ever noticed, but if he arrived unexpectedly I'd dash up and change from the skirt and jumper I was wearing into the nattiest dress or slinkiest pants I had. If he'd warned us beforehand I'd be sure to have my hair done and often, in a fit of excitement, buy something new for the occasion. I suppose it was that when he came he brought a breath of foreign airports and Hiltons with him and the uniform of the 'village' suddenly became dowdy and inadequate.

I didn't envy Dobbie his world, nor was I

seriously discontented with my own. I knew perfectly well that what Tim and I had created together were the lasting things, and that although Dobbie appeared to have everything he really had nothing, except perhaps the playboy's gift of making you feel like a million dollars. It was pleasant after a day of chasing after green Fablon and rugger socks to be given a large bottle of Diorissimo and one of champagne and told you looked prettier than ever; somehow, temporarily you did.

I cannot pinpoint the precise day I conceived the idea of an affair with Dobbie. At one moment it was the vague, un-attainable, romantic idea that I had always had and the next it was something that I knew I was going to do. First I felt very daring, then terribly sorry for Tim, then absolutely obsessed with the idea and how I was to bring it about. There was no hurry. I made the mistake of believing Dobbie could read my thoughts and consequently was aware of my change of attitude towards him. He still kissed me when he came and went, called me darling as if he meant it, as he did everybody, flattered me as he always had, but otherwise remained exactly the same. It became clear that the idea was mine alone and that I would have to construct a plan of how I was going to engineer a situation which would result in the end I was determined, brazenly, to bring about.

Often Tim said to him, jokingly, why don't you get married, Dobbie, settle down? Dobbie would look at me with his lazy eyes and say because I can't find a girl like Liz. He always said things like that, outrageous, complimentary, utterly untrue. When all this started though, almost six months ago now, I talked myself into believing that he meant it, that he really envied Tim, and had been nursing a secret and frustrated desire for me for years. My better judgement told me it wasn't so, I had known Dobbie for long enough. I refused to listen. I continued to build up in my own mind a new picture of Dobbie in which he was passionately in love with me and in which we were carrying on a desperate intrigue beneath Tim's very nose. The more I considered it, and where the notion came from in the first place I don't know, the more determined I became. His visits were few and far between as always but I began to think about him all the time. I imagined that wherever he was he was thinking of me and aching to be home. I pictured us together in a hundred different scenes. His image was with me when Tim and I made love. When he actually did turn up, of course, there was a status quo, no progress had been made except by my imagination. In June I decided I could stand it no longer and that Dobbie would have to know. I did not feel particularly wanton. I was not eighteen but twice that age and knew that most men needed a push before they took the initiative they liked to think their own.

Tim was in the garden tying up the lupins and Dobbie and I were on the floor of the sitting room playing Monopoly with the children. Usually I didn't play those games with them, they bored me. With Dobbie there I didn't mind.

It was terribly hot; the hottest summer that we'd had for years. I still carried the tan for remembrance. The dice seemed to be on my side. I already had Bond Street and Regent Street and needed only Oxford Street to complete my set. Dobbie and I were sprawled on the carpet opposite each other, Dobbie not doing very well with only the Waterworks and Electricity company and some bad debts. Robin put the shaker in my hand. I could see Tim through the French windows on his haunches with the lupins; the hot air had a static quality. I yearned for Dobbie.

'Come on, Mummy,' Diana said, 'it's your go.'

I looked at Dobbie. His eyes met mine for a moment. He went back to making neat rows of the little green houses and red hotels in the property box; then he looked up again, puzzled. It was surprising what one could do with one's eyes. The mirrors of the soul. They were more; the teleprinter and the ticker-tape. I want you to love me, mine said.

He received the message and looked with bewilderment towards the garden where Tim was staggering lopsidedly with the watering can.

Robin gave me a push. 'Mummy! It's your go.'

That was June and it was November. I didn't get Oxford Street, anxious now for the game to be over.

When it was, it seemed to take an eternity, I sent Robin and Diana to the shops for ice cream, although there was a block in the ice-box. Watched by Dobbie I began to clear up the Monopoly.

I wanted him to speak. I had put my cards on the table and having made the effort I felt I could not, with any pretensions to modesty, do more.

'Liz.'

'Yes.' He was quite edible in his navy blue Italian shirt.

'Is anything the matter?'

'In what way?'

'You and Tim?'

I shook my head and stacked the cardboard property cards with exaggerated neatness, fastening them with a rubber band.

'I'm off to the Middle East in the morning.'

He was changing the subject which had scarcely been broached.

'I know.'

He lit a cigarette and I realised that he knew I was not completely across the river and was giving me time to go back. I'd once read an article in a woman's magazine. It cautioned young girls against going out with married men because they would not be satisfied with holding hands in the pictures.

I was collecting the symbols we played with. I had the ship and the car and the silver thimble. Dobbie handed me the aeroplane. I knew very well what was involved and had no intention of turning back.

'How long will be you away?'

'Three weeks, four.'

He stood up, looking at me. I think he was trying to decide. I knew what the trouble was. He looked out into the garden. Tim was going for more water.

'Tim will be wanting tea.' I put the Monopoly away and straightened my dress. I had bought it especially for Dobbie. 'Iced coffee perhaps. It's too hot for tea.'

Dobbie was watching me. I had set the wheels in motion and now I was embarrassed. I was not eighteen, I had told myself, but I felt as if I was.

'You're staying for dinner? Supper really, just cold and salads, the heat…'

'I have an appointment in town.'

60

A horrid thought struck me. He was running away. He didn't care two hoots. I had made myself cheap. He was laughing; sorry for Tim; snubbing me.

'See you when you get back then.'

I almost ran into the kitchen to prepare the iced coffee. He followed me. I was standing by the fridge. He lifted my hair and kissed the back of my neck, keeping his mouth there for along time. I glanced out of the window but Tim was busy with the hose now.

'I've often wondered about your neck.'

I leaned against him, a hundred nerve endings feeling him and the summer and the infidelity of it all, everything you thought was neatly tied up in a box.

'I think one should consider,' Dobbie said. I knew his eyes were on the garden.

'One has.'

'You mean...?'

I nodded.

'How long?'

'Long.'

'You're an extraordinary girl, Liz.'

Tim came in, mopping his forehead, for a drink.

There was a banging on the door and I realised that the bathwater had grown cold, my fingertips pale, and skin wrinkled.

'What is it?'

'The Salvation Army,' Mrs MacSweeney

said. 'They left an envelope.'

I needed salvation.

'You'll find half-a-crown on the dressing-table.'

I pulled the plug out unwilling to let the water go.

Four

What *did* one wear?

I held my dressing-gown around me. In spite of the central heating the bedroom didn't seem terribly hot. The fog seemed to get everywhere. I stood in front of my underwear shelf. The obvious choice of course was black. In films they always wore black. I don't remember a seduction sequence in any other colour. Rejecting it as too obvious I settled for champagne trimmed with champagne lace; more subtle.

I put the underwear on, then my dressing-gown again over it and sat down in front of the mirror. Having examined it thoroughly I came to the conclusion that I was in good face. I was not beautiful. In spite of Robin and Diana, or perhaps because of, my figure was nothing to be ashamed of, just a shade too much over the hips perhaps but not like Martha, poor Martha who insisted on wearing trousers on Sunday mornings and really shouldn't. My face was a victim of the moon. At the beginning of the month I was tolerably pretty, quite satisfied with myself, happy; as it drew to its close my features, nothing in themselves, faded to ordinariness. An undefinable plainness crept over them forming a mask I hated, but could not change. This was a good day.

I often longed for that sort of beauty that was indestructible; the Madonna kind that was independent of mood or of the moon, that looked good first thing in the morning or in any hat no matter how hideous; beauty of the non-fade variety that you saw once in every crowd and made you wonder why you bothered to compete. I would have liked to have been born with that, you needed nothing more, or failing that a voice. To open your mouth and hear heavenly sounds emerge; sounds that caused listeners to settle into an embarrassed stillness; to know that you had made them. There was a gift.

I took up the jar of moisturising cream to make the most of what I had.

Dobbie always sent postcards to the children. After he left for the Middle East I got through the hot days as best I could and waited for them. Would they be the same? Would he send a message only I would understand, keyed to receive it? Was he laughing? When it came it had a picture of a camel and a little black-eyed Arab boy in ragged trousers, and was addressed to Robin who collected them and had an entire shoe-box full. 'They are not as nice when you get close,' Dobbie wrote. 'Covered in flies. I suppose that applies to everything. Best love to Mummy and Daddy, Uncle Dobbie.' That was all. Could I read anything into the parable of the camels and the flies? I wasn't sure. Perhaps he meant it would be better if we kept our distance and our illusions. Perhaps he meant nothing of the sort, and it was my over-sensitive mind drawing incorrect conclusions. After the camels there was one more. A market in Marrakesh. It said 'Tell Mummy just like Betterfare!' and that he was bringing Diana, to whom it was addressed this time – Dobbie was scrupulously fair – a necklace made of amber. Betterfare was our local supermarket. Even I, in my highly susceptible condition, could draw no esoteric message from the analogy. I had to wait, burning with impatience.

June dragged into July; the end of term when we were to take the children to Italy was almost in sight. Dobbie must be back from the Middle East. Had he decided not to get in touch? Perhaps I had lost, Tim too, a friend of many years' standing. Because of the kiss on the neck and my intuition, which could usually be relied on, I rejected these suppositions. I waited for an afternoon, when Tim was out, and before it was time for the children to come home from school, and rang his flat. I felt nervous. I told myself it was only Dobbie; old Dobbie. The old Dobbie, by my own machinations no longer existed. One could only go forward. A woman answered. She said Hyde Park two four two nine like a cat who had been at the cream. I put the receiver down without saying anything and decided I would make Tim cold fruit soup which he adored for dinner. I refused, absolutely refused to think about Dobbie. The incident, and it really was rather a stupid incident, childish in its way, was over.

I was waiting next morning for Harrods' Soft Furnishings to call me back about the new fitted spread for Robin's room when he rang.

'Yes!' I said, crossly. I'd waited twenty minutes and wanted to go out.

'Liz?'

'Dobbie.' I felt my face suffuse with red thinking of my call of yesterday. 'You got back,' I said fatuously.

'I've been back a couple of days. I had some business to attend to.'

I bet.

'I've a spare Centre Court seat for Wednesday. Interested?'

I'd been out with Dobbie before but only with the children, a cosy family party as it were.

'Very.'

Dobbie was a keen tennis player and a very good one.

'I'll pick you up at 1.30.'

'Come for dinner on Thursday,' I said.

'We're off to Italy at the weekend.'

'I'd like to.'

'Did you enjoy your trip?'

'I think something will come of it.'

Of course he wasn't a starry-eyed traveller, and thought of the globe in terms of what it would yield to one Arthur Dobson.

'I'll tell you about it when I see you.'

He was in a hurry.

'Tim and the kids all right?'

'Fine.'

'I'll bring their presents. Tell Robin I've an Arab head-dress. 'Bye now.'

'Goodbye.'

I put the receiver down. The phone rang again almost immediately.

'Mrs Westbury? Harrods Soft Furnishing...' I no longer cared.

I told Tim over dinner. Why not? Dobbie was our oldest friend.

'Good show,' he said. Tim had never quite forgotten the Air Force. 'Some people have all the luck.'

He meant Wimbledon in the middle of the week while he had to sweat it out in the office. I can't say I felt sorry for him, only amazed that he couldn't read what was in my mind; how you could know someone as well as Tim and I knew each other, live side by side and yet not know one single bit. I was on the verge of deceiving him and he hadn't an inkling because I was able to control my face and endow it with its customary expression. For all I knew he had murder in his heart. It was impossible to tell. You knew – nothing.

'I hope the weather holds,' Tim said.

It did. I don't think I have ever been so hot. Clothes were no problem. I had a new navy linen dress Dobbie hadn't seen, with its own jacket trimmed with white braid. I rejected navy blue accessories and decided on white then was worried in case I'd overdone the touches of white, a solecism against which the fashion pundits were always warning. I dressed with the excitement of a child going to a birthday but when I was ready, nearly three-quarters of an hour too early, knew that the effect was suitable and attractive. Looking out of the dining-room window I waited for Dobbie. At 1.30 exactly his green Mercedes swept into the drive. He seemed to get out before it had stopped.

At the front door he kissed me, no more no less than usual, looking desperately handsome and brown from his trip. He wore sun-glasses so I couldn't see his expression.

'Ready?'

'Yes.' I picked up my handbag from the hall table.

'Let's go.'

The heat in the drive felt more Mediterranean than English. It was shimmering up off the asphalt. We walked round the car to the other side and Dobbie opened the door. There was a girl sitting in the middle of the front seat and I was transfixed; I think open-mouthed.

'This is Catherine,' Dobbie said. 'Catherine meet Liz.'

She held out a black-gloved hand and smiled a cover-girl smile.

'Forgive me not getting out. These skirts make it quite a manoeuvre.'

She wore a black sleeveless shift, completely plain, black patent shoes on sensational legs, black bag, black glasses. On her honey-blonde head was a white pique beret. I felt like a Christmas tree with my umpteen touches of white and knew my navy blue two-piece was desperately ordinary. Not only that; she had the edge on me by ten years or more. I had never known Dobbie cruel. Could I plead a headache, stomach-ache, indigestion?'

I shook the hand, returning the smile, and Dobbie said: 'In you get.' I hadn't the strength to do anything else but collapse on to the seat which was hot and feel my damp arm touch her cool one. She emanated *Je Reviens;* probably a present from Dobbie.

The only thing that can be said for the afternoon is that it passed. A Czech with a backhand like a tornado won the men's singles. Royalty arrived and we went through the bowing routine. We had strawberries and cream without having to queue up.

Catherine was as nice as she was beautiful. I hated her. Dobbie was strictly fair dividing his attention between us. I never remember feeling quite so hot or humiliated.

When they dropped me off at 6.30 I didn't invite them in for a drink.

'See you tomorrow,' I said to Dobbie. 'Don't be late. It's Tim's early night.'

'Do you still want me?' I saw the eyebrows come up over the dark glasses he hadn't removed all afternoon.

'Why not?' I said, although there was every reason.

I said goodbye to Catherine, still cool as a cucumber and chic and she said it was nice meeting me. Cattily I didn't return the compliment.

Tim was home. He envied me my lovely afternoon and I took all my sticky clothes off angrily, giving a kick to the navy two-piece which fell on to the floor and got under the shower.

It was Tim who provided the impetus for the next step in the progress of my affair with Dobbie.

He came for dinner at the usual time. I wore a pink cotton dress not caring after Catherine and gave him beef which I knew he hated to punish him. He talked shares with Tim. Halfway through dinner Tim said what's the matter Liz you're very quiet and I said it must be the heat not looking at Dobbie. The telephone rang and Tim went to answer it and I made a great to-do over the apple pie and cream so that we didn't have to talk.

When Tim came back he said he had to go out for a while after dinner to visit a client but that he wouldn't be very long and he was sure we could amuse ourselves. Had it happened on the stage you would have said it was contrived.

After Tim had gone I took a long time clearing the table and putting the dishes in the dishwasher. I wiped the Formica tops thoroughly, swept the floor, wrapped the remains of the pie in tinfoil and leaving the kitchen immaculate, I did not always, carried the tray of coffee into the sitting-room. Dobbie was smoking and reading the newspaper with his feet up on a footstool.

I gave him his coffee.

'Did you enjoy your dinner?'

'No. Hated it.'

'Good.'

'What was the idea?'

'Punishment for Catherine.'

'Sorry about that. I suppose it was a bit clumsy.'

'Downright ham-handed. Unnecessary to boot. You could have told me you and Catherine... I could have taken the hint.'

'But Catherine and I are not. Anyway I did it for Tim. Tim trusts me with you. I wanted to put you off. I was doing my duty. Did I succeed?'

'No.'

'Good.'

'It was cruel to bring Catherine.'

'I apologise.'

'Less young, less chic; you can't be with two children and a home to run. The change is insidious. When you come up against someone like Catherine you realise just how far the metamorphosis has gone.'

'I love you more.'

'You love Catherine then?'

'Ships that pass in the night.'

'How interesting your nights must be.'

'Probably no more interesting than yours. Yours and Tim's.'

'Why do you keep bringing Tim into it?'

'He trusts me with you. Seriously, Liz. I don't notice anything different. You and Tim.'

'There isn't anything.'

'I don't understand then.'

'I can't help you. I don't really understand myself except that this has nothing to do with Tim. I keep thinking about you. It's something I have to get out of my system.'

'I don't think he'd be terribly pleased.'

'He wouldn't know. It would probably be short-lived.'

'Playing with fire, Liz. You never know what kind of a conflagration you're starting.'

'Dobbie, if you aren't interested just say so.'

'You know quite well I've always wanted you. Been half in love in a way; sharing you with Tim without the responsibilities.'

'Sometimes I think it's the responsibilities that kill.' I handed him his coffee and the sugar, coloured crystals.

'They're supposed to enrich.'

'Tell me what you see enriching about mortgages and a chip in the cooker and the roots of our poplar tree undermining the foundations of the house next door.'

'I've never known you so cynical.'

'You've never known me. You've watched me do my act, Tim and the children...'

'I thought it was part of you.'

'If you play it for long enough it becomes part of you. Only part. There's another part though, the part that's free to roam. It does too. We live in a divided world; what we're doing and we're thinking; women at any rate. They aren't the same you know. If you want out just say so.'

'I suppose I should get up and go. Regards to Tim etcetera, called away.'

'You aren't going to?'

I was afraid for a moment.

'No.'

Suddenly it was over. The situation I had

dreamed on, though over night and day was under way. Dobbie stood up and I stood up too, the coffee cooling. For a moment we were immobilised on the black and white carpet I had chosen for not showing the dirt, hedged by the Liberty's coffee table and the black sofa with its scatter cushions. I felt disgusted with myself for a moment only then that this was what I had been waiting for and we moved together. It was everything I expected and transported me as I had forgotten one could be transported. I didn't think I could wait until we came back from Italy to see him again and had wild ideas of sending myself a telegram to come home, from Martha or someone, but of course it would be impossible. In his arms I tried not to think of Tim and make comparisons but just enjoy it. For the first time I sensed the danger of the whole thing and that it wasn't going to be quite as easy as I thought. My legs felt weak.

When we released each other, with reluctance, Dobbie said: 'If you like we could call that one on the house; without prejudice.'

There was time still to make a joke of it, he meant, for Tim and I to close the doors of our nest snug with Robin and Diana and an occasional visit from Dobbie to liven us all up.

In reply I put my arms round his neck and let everything else fade. He was like granite, not like Tim, slight when you held him.

The conflagration was truly under way. I moved from him feeling odd still in a way I hadn't for years and Dobbie lit a cigarette from the slim gold case inside which I knew he carried a photograph of himself, younger and slimmer as a Wing-Commander.

'It looks as though we're in business,' he said. 'What shall we do until Tim comes back.'

I knew what he meant. To keep ourselves occupied. There was an invisible magnet pulling us together. I didn't look at him so that I could stay on the other side of the room.

'Talk, I suppose.' My hand was shaking, the coffee cold. 'Tell me about the Middle East.'

The door opened and Diana came in yawning. She and Robin had had an early supper because they were doing *Great Expectations* on television and they wanted to watch. I'd forgotten about them.

'Hallo, Uncle Dobbie.'

'Good play?'

'Mm.'

'I was going to tell Mummy about my trip.'

She went naturally to sit on his knee. Suddenly there was something wrong. I went into the kitchen to take the dishes out of the dishwasher although I usually left them until morning.

It was the divided world again; the greater part belonging to Tim and the children, the lesser, which I knew I would never relinquish, to myself. I was aware of this dichotomy then, when I saw my child sitting on Dobbie's knee confusing the separate images and I was aware of it now as I sat before the mirror on the day of the culmination, or perhaps the real beginning of my affair with Dobbie.

I had made up my face with precision while allowing my thoughts to wander. Downstairs I could hear Mrs Mac busy with the Hoover and remembered that before I left I must sort out the washing and put it in the machine; she wouldn't touch it, too complicated she said, hers was simpler.

In the bathroom I took the mascara in its slim blue box from the cupboard above the mirror. The light was better here than in the bedroom and I could see the triangular web of lines at the corners of my eyes against which Harrods sold a cream at thirty-five guineas a jar. I wasn't that foolish realising their inevitability but I suppose my eyes were slightly misted with the hope that blinded the others because only last week I had paid fourteen and six for a tube of something that promised to make the crow's feet less evident.

Looking critically I thought perhaps I had

plastered it on a bit for first thing only I wouldn't have the chance to come home again before going to Dobbie's. It may only have been that I was slightly pale with fright, anticipation, and that the make-up sat awkwardly upon the pallor.

I was holding up a black wool dress and a tweed suit and looking out of the window trying to decide which, to take off, I told myself nervously, when Mrs Mac came in and said you'll want to wrap up it's nasty. She was holding something in her hand.

It was the Limoges ashtray Tim had brought back from a business trip to Paris. It was in two halves.

It came to pieces in her hands Mrs Mac said, naturally she didn't even touch it.

I took the two pieces of pink and white china. The ashtray was pretty but of no particular value. I was glad I did not believe in symbolism.

Five

Even on this day of intrigue the shopping had to be done. Thus, as always, women were reduced, cut down to size, had greatness whittled away. Not that I was contemplating an increase in stature; a decrease, morally speaking. It would have been the same though if I had been. Could you be great, painting, writing, while around you mouths were open for food? Mountain climbing certainly not; athletics, a few made it, exchanging dedication for life. We were foiled at every turn; by margarine and assorted biscuits and quarters of tea. *Après moi le déluge.* First there was dinner to think of.

My relationship with our local supermarket was of the love/hate variety. I shopped there because of the time saved by being able to get a diversity of items under one roof. Often though I'd come out with caviare-style lump-fish roe or a jar of lime pickle, having gone in for an innocent loaf.

I don't know who chose the music to which we rejected and selected our purchases but imagined that the tunes were chosen for their soporific rather than aesthetic qualities. One had to stop oneself from a hypnotic trance induced by a purring rendering of *Night and Day*, from reaching out, dream-like, for tins of ground jeera or push-button lavatory deodorant one had had no intention of buying. I hated the big brothers I knew were sitting behind the glass panel high on the back wall which on our unsuspecting side was mirror, spying on me, waiting for me to slip the baked beans into my own basket instead of theirs and cover them up with my scarf (shoplifters always had scarves). I was not, as they had calculated, much good at sales resistances. To the lilting rhythm of *The Skater's Waltz* I invariably succumbed to the juicy appeal of canned apricots at a reduction of three-pence and raspberry jelly for Robin, three for the price of two.

Today they were playing *The Lady is a Tramp* interrupted at intervals by a raucous voice calling, 'Mr Calthorpe, telephone, please'. I walked resolutely past the *Potage aux Champignons*, reduced to a shilling, towards the meat and poultry at the far end of the store. At the delicatessen I faltered, Odysseus lured off course by the pungent odour of ripe Camembert; no Circe displayed her charms more invitingly. On the counter the farmhouse Brie on its bed of straw oozed creamily, the shiny black olives, Tim's favourite, glistened against a background of hanging Bologna sausages. I hesitated, to a seductive rendering of *Bewitched, Bothered and Bewildered* (someone had a sense of humour), then thought that by tonight I would be technically guilty of the offence I had already committed mentally and was honest enough, honest! not to allow myself to bring offerings in expiation; not that Tim would know; would ever know.

Down the aisle between the fish fingers, Robin inevitably remarked he didn't know a fish had fingers, and the cream, double and single, then a smart about turn, catching my shins on someone's wretched basket as I remembered flaky pastry and that I was going to put the steak into a pie. Tim of course thought I still made my own pastry, rolling it and putting it into the fridge for five minutes then rolling it again and had no idea that it came called 'Roll-Easy' all prepared in a tinfoil packet. I put one into my basket and somebody said hallo Liz and it was Monica clutching her basket with a bottle of Handy-Andy, fourpence off, sticking out and a jumbo tin of grapefruit juice, and Olga Tindal clutching hers. Most of the girls in the village hunted in pairs. Neither term, girl nor village, was strictly accurate. All of us were veering towards the forties, some more some less, and where we lived was one of those high-class suburbs not far from town which we thought we endowed with a little character, or perhaps it was because of the gossip that went on and there was plenty of that, by calling the twenty- or thirty-odd streets with their larger or smaller detached houses our 'village'.

They were both looking at me and I couldn't think why then I remembered I had on my black coat with the mink tie Tim had bought me for my birthday and stiletto heels and that it must look a bit odd with the wire basket and the flaky pastry.

'I'm going up to town,' I said, dropping two little pieces of my alibi. 'Meeting Martha for lunch.'

'Have they any frozen raspberries?' Monica said. 'There was a recipe in *Queen*, I was reading it in the hairdresser's and copied it out on the back of my cheque-book.' She fumbled in her handbag and produced it. 'Frozen raspberries, unsweetened, meringue case.'

'You put a little cornflour and vinegar into the meringue mixture,' Olga said, 'it's called a Pavlova.'

A woman wheeling a trolley piled with tins pushed by with a toddler saying, 'Mum! Mum! Mummy!'

'Anyway,' Monica was bent over the fridge, 'it doesn't look as if they have any raspberries. Gooseberries or strawberries. Reggie hates gooseberries and strawberries bring me out in bumps.'

'Mushrooms do that to me,' Olga said. She picked up a packet of frozen herring-roes.

'Reggie won't touch frozen fish,' Monica said. 'He doesn't mind vegetables.'

'Can he tell the difference?' Olga said helping herself to peas and sprouts. 'I give Archie roes on toast twice a week for breakfast and I've never enlightened him.'

'Reggie's very fussy about that sort of thing.' I caught Olga's eye. 'He gets it from his mother. She's one of the old-fashioned sort, goes to the butcher's and prods it all. If it wasn't labelled I wouldn't know one cut from the next. I got a chart from the *Daily Telegraph* once and hung it on the larder door. It had a bull, coloured and divided into sections. The trouble was I couldn't understand the key. Are you coming for coffee?'

She meant the 'Papagallo' where most of the village could be found at eleven o'clock sitting at the tables by the window shredding the reputations of all who passed and eating Danish pastries with Saxin in the cappuccino.

'I want to look for a dress for Pamela's wedding,' I said.

'I haven't a thing,' Olga said. 'Tessa's getting herself up in red velvet, she simply hasn't a clue. I suppose she thinks as mother of the bride she has to be outstanding.'

'She'll be that all right,' Monica said. 'Have you sent a present yet?'

'Can I come by?' The woman with the loaded trolley and the toddler was retracing her steps.

'Mum, Mum, Mummy,' the child said.

'Oh, shut up, do!'

'It's supposed to be one way,' Olga pointed out.

The woman looked at her ocelot jacket and pushed on.

'I thought one of those Pyrex oven sets, but Reggie says something silver,' Monica said. 'I was thinking of the cleaning.'

'You've always *got* silver,' Olga said. She had a maid to clean it.

'There's so much to choose,' Monica said. 'Do you remember when we got married?'

I thought of the plain white cups and saucers and the ghastly utility bed.

A tall man in a bowler hat who had taken one of the very tiny baskets and looked ludicrous said: 'I wonder if you could tell me where I can find the Puffed Wheat?' to Olga. Olga smiling, gave him the works, eyes, teeth, everything. I think it was a reflex stimulated by the male and came naturally. 'Over by the wall,' she said.

We had all got married within a few years of the end of the war. Our wedding dresses had been made of any material we were lucky enough to find and not of our choice and our homes had been similarly furnished. Pamela Talbot had the world at her feet; in our day there had been no coloured oven-to-table ware, king-sized bed linen, Terylene eiderdowns. It was a world we had almost forgotten.

'Did you hear about my biff?' Monica said. 'In the car. Reggie's furious. I was taking the corner of Chestnut and Beech and this fellow came round absolutely on the wrong side, not stopping and of course I went smack into him. He wasn't a bit nice but fortunately the postman was on the corner emptying the box and saw everything and said it wasn't my fault. I don't think Reggie believed him and anyway the wing is a horrid mess and I shan't have the car for three weeks.'

We were lost without our cars. None of us was used to standing at bus stops and couldn't get through the day if we had to. If the women in the village didn't have their own cars they used their husbands' while they went to town on the tube; there was nowhere to park anyway. Most of us had children who had to be taken and fetched if not from school to music or dancing or Guides or Cubs or extra coaching. When we were small we hadn't been chauffeured anywhere, but our children were used to it. They regarded with horror any distance to be footed greater than half a mile.

'I just grazed one of the doors a few weeks ago,' Olga said. 'No, it must have been last month because it was the day before Claire's birthday and I was dashing out to buy place-cards. It was the tiniest little graze but apparently it had to be resprayed, thirty pounds, but Archie knew a chap who does it privately and he took the whole door off and it's like new for half that money.'

'They just put it on,' Monica said. 'Like with the television. We lost the picture on the bedroom one, and the chap said new tube, tube's gone, and you don't really know if it has or not.'

'That's why Archie rents ours.'

'It's far more expensive, Reggie says.'

'Yes but at least you get twenty-four-hour service.'

I wondered what we should have for dessert and thought perhaps ice-cream and then that it would melt because I wasn't going home and picked up a double cream and reminded myself to get a tin of fruit cocktail on the way out.

'I have to get some meat,' I said.

'We have too.'

We shuffled with our two lots of baskets each, our own and Betterfare's, towards the end canopied counters, where butchers in spotless white aprons presided over the tripe and chuck steak. The cuts were arranged prettily in plastic containers covered with cellophane and looked like the pretend food with which as children we had once played dolls' houses. I hesitated between a pound-and-a-half and two pounds. Sometimes the children came in ravenous and sometimes not hungry at all. Robin often went to bed with just some cereal. I decided on the two pounds, I could always finish up what was left for lunch tomorrow, and put it in the wire basket. Then I thought, no. The money I saved would buy the fruit cocktail and a pound-and-a-half would do, because of the pastry, I'd forgotten about that. I put it back, watching the glass panel above with guilt, and took the smaller cut instead. Monica took sausages which was typical and Olga lamb cutlets which was also typical and which I knew she would serve with paper frills in a silver entrée dish.

'I have to go,' I said, 'or I'll be late.'

'Coffee,' Monica said. 'I need some ground.'

'Cheerio. Tell Martha we're expecting her for bridge tomorrow.' Olga waved a plastic tray containing half a chicken.

The time you saved in the supermarket you lost trying to get out again. There were queues at all the check-out points. I joined the shortest, three people coming in no time behind me, then I remembered the tin of fruit cocktail and decided not to bother or I'd lose my place. There must be something in the larder. The woman I stood behind had only a tin of sweet corn and a swiss roll and some steel-wool in her basket and I thought that's good she won't take long. We shuffled slowly up to the counter. I put a packet of Maltesers and a milk chocolate flake for Robin and Diana into my basket and a box of matches exactly as Betterfare had intended I should. I got my purse out ready as the woman ahead of me put her basket down in front of the girl who was operating the till. The plastic label on her bosom said Miss Jenkins and that she was at my service. She had ginger hair and false eyelashes and I think what was intended to be the Cleopatra look. She pressed the buttons smartly, one-and-a-penny for the swiss roll and ninepence for the steel-wool and one-and-six for the sweet corn. She had a long red finger-nail on the total button when the woman said oh no the sweet corn was one-and-fourpence-halfpenny. Miss Jenkins up-ended the tin and one-and-six was stamped indelibly in blue. The woman said on the shelf was a ticket that said one-and-fourpence-halfpenny. Miss Jenkins looked at the till, which was irrevocable, and sighed and waited. The woman waited too and I shuffled with impatience and so did the people behind beginning to get curious. The woman, sticking to her guns, said I would like to get it cleared up, flushing but only slightly. Miss Jenkins still saying nothing but looking daggers whined 'Mr Weller, check-out please!' into her microphone and settled down to stare vacantly into space. I glanced across at the other queues but they were now quite long and it was pointless losing my place. I was annoyed because I still had to go to the greengrocer's and give an order. Mr Weller in a blue overall hurried across and said what's the trouble Miss Jenkins and the woman explained quite politely about the sweet corn. Mr Weller shepherded her away to the place where she had found the offending article and we all breathed a sigh of relief. It turned out to be premature because having started the addition, but not rung up a total, Miss Jenkins was powerless to take the money for our goods no matter how much we chaffed and champed. A young man with a loaf of bread put down one-and-three on the counter and pushed his way through and Miss Jenkins looked at it doubtfully then decided to accept it putting it neatly on one side. In any case the young man had already gone and you could see she'd had enough trouble for one morning. Eventually the woman came back shepherded by Mr Weller and said nicely to Miss Jenkins that she had had the matter satisfactorily explained. The one-and-fourpence-halfpenny referred to the chilli-peppers on the shelf below. Miss Jenkins pressed the total button extracting the paper receipt with its purple figures and we all pushed merrily on.

I could see it was going to be one of those mornings. Somebody had parked his car not two inches from my front bumper and there was a van about eighteen inches away behind. I was sure Tim would have managed, he was wonderful about that sort of thing, but I might just as well attempt to jump over the moon. I put the Betterfare stuff in the boot and noticed I had Diana's pleated skirt, I would have to drop that into the cleaner's, and decided that by the time I had been to the greengrocer's the person who had been so inconsiderate might have finished shopping and moved his car. If not I should just have to sit there and hoot.

Of course you could get vegetables in the supermarket but when we needed potatoes and heavy things I gave an order once a week at Smart's. Mr Smart had very large false teeth and was always grinning trying to keep his end up as a small shopkeeper gradually being driven to the wall by Betterfare and Brown's Self-Service and others in the village gradually converting. It was only his mouth which smiled ingratiatingly though, you could see his eyes were tired. There was a greyness about him and you knew he had to get up about half-past four in the morning to go to market.

'Good morning, Mrs Westbury.' Grin.

'And how's Mrs Westbury today? Order?'

'Yes, please.'

'I'll get a book.'

His window was set out temptingly, the apples polished. Anticipating experiments, our cosy dinners for eight or ten, he kept a stock of artichokes, aubergines, avocado pears, saving us a journey to town.

'Potatoes,' I said, 'ten pounds...'

'Edwards or Whites?'

I looked at him doubtfully.

'Whites are a better peeling.'

'Whites then. Two pounds of onions, a pound of carrots, a pound of tomatoes, a quarter of mushrooms, medium cabbage...'

'Oranges? Bananas? Grapefruit?' Pencil poised.

I picked up a grapefruit from a stack feeling the weight of it and caught sight of myself in the mirror that ran along the side of the shop. All dressed up in black for Dobbie with my mink tie, holding aloft a grapefruit like the Statue of Liberty.

'Very juicy,' Mr Smart said.

'What's that?'

'Juicy. Thin-skinned.'

'Oh yes. I'll have two.'

'And the next?'

The car was still wedged. I hate anything mechanical feeling completely inadequate. It was fairly new, blue and white with plastic-covered seats. I got in, you could still smell the newness, and hooted twice hoping the owner of the red Mini in front would hear. We were outside Stapleton's and I could see several little queues, they always made you line up for butter and cheese and bacon separately which was why I seldom went so perhaps she was in there. I was sure it was a woman because no man would have been so stupid. A few people turned round at the noise, mildly curious. There was a tap on the window and it was Heather Skinner and for once I was quite pleased to see her feeling rather alone in my embarrassing situation.

I lowered the window by the passenger seat. 'I'm stuck.'

'What a rotten thing to do,' Heather said. She had on a purply tweed suit, red stockings and no coat and was carrying what looked like a mop, just its head wrapped in brown paper.

'A new mop,' she said holding it aloft. 'Binkie chewed the head off the old one, little terror.'

Heather had no children but a succession of cats and dogs which I'm sure were far more trouble and certainly received more attention; meat cooked twice daily and liver chopped up, the smell was revolting when you went into her house, and that sort of thing.

'Look, you start backing and forwarding,'

Heather said heartily standing there with the mop like Boadicea, 'and I'll see you out.'

'I think it's impossible.'

'Not at all. Little by little and easy does it.'

Older than most of us I remembered that Heather had been a driver in the W.A.A.F I turned on the ignition and put myself in her hands.

Back and forth and back and forth and back and forth. Apart from being exhausted and hot and uncomfortable I was fed up with the whole affair. There was quite a little crowd on the pavement, most with shopping baskets, all offering advice.

'One more and you'll make it,' Heather said looking professionally at the front bumper.

An elderly man with a brown paper carrier came out of Stapleton's. He poked his head in my window smelling of tobacco.

'I'm terribly sorry, am I in your way?'

I opened my mouth to let forth the stream of abuse I had been preparing which was peppered with words such as inconsiderate, foolish, incompetent, and selfish.

'I'll move it straight away,' he said taking out his keys. 'I was going to the Victoria Wine Company for a bottle of stone ginger but I'll move the little bus first shall I?'

I pulled out into the High Street feeling stupid in a way for having got so worked up. I hated the car feeling it was my enemy and often out to make me look ridiculous.

People were crossing to and fro in the High Street standing on the islands with parcels or baskets on wheels and spilling over the zebra crossings which always gave me nightmares in case I knocked somebody down. Reaching the traffic lights, hemmed in by a bus on one side and a petrol lorry on the other, I turned right and joined the stream of miscellaneous traffic going to town.

Six

The holiday in Italy had been a success, paradoxically, I suppose, because knowing that I had Dobbie at home waiting for me I had gone out of my way to be pleasant to Tim. Nothing annoyed me. I had something so exciting to go home to that I could afford to be magnanimous, and the three weeks passed in a kind of expectant limbo. We hired a car and toured for a bit then finished up to recuperate at Venice Lido. I stood with respect in St Peter's admiring the hideous baldachino and thought of Dobbie. I thought of him crossing the dusty Piazza Santa Croce hand in hand with Tim. I lay face down on the sand on the scorching Lido listening to the shouts of Robin and Diana in the water and wondered how it would be.

I'd told Dobbie when we'd be home and he'd made a note of it in his diary saying he'd be in touch.

We came back at the end of August to find the garden overgrown, Tim hadn't been there to see to it, and everything looking rather dehydrated because there had been no rain.

In the house the first thing I did was to

make a quick tour to see if Mrs Mac had been in and doing all she should. The net curtains looked clean and fresh and I smelled them to make sure they were. She'd washed the carpets and the paint work everywhere and seemed really to have been hard at it while we were taking it easy, although the sightseeing had been hard work in Italy. I had brought her a bag from the straw market in Florence and a silk scarf I thought would go well with her winter coat. Mrs Mac had done a coach tour of the Bavarian Alps in the spring and had brought me back a wonderful wooden nutcracker made by hand and a large bottle of Eau-de-Cologne which still stood embarrassingly unused on my dressing table; if there was one smell I couldn't stand it was that. I hoped she would find her presents adequate. The post was piled neatly on the dining-room table and with the cases still in the hall Tim was sorting it. The children were prowling round looking at everything and leaving a trail of comics, which they'd read in the plane, and opened tubes of wine-gums and the straw hat Diana hadn't let go of since Milan. Soon the house, which had seemed a bit strange and expectant when we arrived, began to get the familiar lived-in look.

Tim finished the post, there were a few for me, Harrods' catalogue and notices of a

Bring-and-Buy Sale and a Luncheon and a Fashion Show all in aid of various charities and which I supposed I would support, but nothing of any interest.

Tim collected up all the envelopes in his methodical way and said what's to eat, and Robin who was pulling his underwater goggles out of one of the cases said yes I'm starving and I realised it wasn't a question of sitting at a laid table and reading the menu but of preparing something myself and that we were really home.

The next day was Tuesday and Tim went off to the office looking brown and fit and the children to the swimming pool, it was still hot. I was left among the debris of dirty sports-shirts and shorts and light dresses feeling let down and resentful that the Adriatic was no longer outside the window, and waiting to hear from Dobbie.

He rang while I was beating the eggs for the Norwegian Cream I was making for dessert. I hadn't heard the phone because of the mixer and Mrs Mac answered it and said Mr Dobson. I switched off the beaters and ran to the telephone in the hall then decided I had better take it upstairs. I asked Mrs Mac to put the receiver down, then thought that was a stupid thing to have done. Dobbie often phoned after all and now she might think something was up but it was too late.

I said 'Hallo Dobbie' and waited for the

click. He said: 'Hallo, Liz. Have a good holiday?' Then I heard it and the bedroom door was shut so that was all right and the sound of his voice made me disintegrate.

'When can I see you?' he said.

I said: 'Any time.' And then thought that was ridiculous because the children were still on holiday and I'd promised to take them to Kew Gardens that week, and shopping for winter uniform which they'd grown out of and shoes, a nightmare with Diana. There were a hundred and one other things too which had piled up while we had been away.

'What about lunch on Thursday?'

Thursday was to have been Diana's shoe morning and I'd promised her lunch in town but it would have to be Thursday because Wednesday was uniforms and Friday was the day we'd settled on for Kew.

'Thursday would be fine,' I said. I would have somehow to square it with Diana and make it fine.

'One o'clock then at Overton's?'

'Not Overton's, Dobbie.' Everyone went there and I was sure to bump into someone I knew.

'Where do you suggest then? I'm at your disposal.'

I tried to think. All the restaurants I knew the girls in the village knew too.

'You could come up to the flat if you like,'

Dobbie said. 'I can have something sent in.'

But I wasn't ready for that.

'I'll tell you what,' he said, 'there's a place in King's Road. It's called "the Porterhouse" and it isn't bad at all. It's right by Kinnerton Street and there's usually somewhere to park.'

'I'll find it.'

'Thursday then.' He sounded busy.

'Goodbye.'

Downstairs in the kitchen I looked at the eggs I had been whipping but they seemed not to have sunk. I switched the mixer on once more and took the castor sugar out of the cupboard and thought how difficult it was all going to be. I was prepared to go through with what I had planned but I wasn't prepared for Tim to find out. I loved and respected him too much. Suddenly the whole of London seemed too small and I couldn't think of a single place where I was unlikely to bump into someone I knew who would say to Tim I ran into Dobbie and Liz having lunch... Not that there was anything wrong in my lunching with Dobbie and Tim would never dream anything was amiss but of course if it happened more than once... The eggs were dry and left the side of the bowl clean. I added the sugar slowly. It was not going to be easy.

Thursday's problem was resolved more simply than I had expected. Diana was invited to spend the day with Penelope Haynes from school. Penelope lived in Knightsbridge so it was all quite convenient. I could drop her there after the shoes and the Haynes' would bring her home later.

I have said it was a nightmare buying shoes for Diana. In actual fact it was worse. It was a kind of three-point pitched battle between Diana, myself and the salesgirl, who tried hard to please us both and ended up, through no fault of her own, by pleasing neither.

The trouble was that both Diana and myself had fixed ideas about the shoes we were to buy and the ideas did not tally. In Diana's mind were pointed-toed court shoes, bad for the feet, with a tiny heel; in mine were sensible light-weight weekenders with a single strap suitable for a girl of twelve. It wasn't that Diana was unreasonable. She was quite an amenable child. She was afraid of looking (a) a nit, (b) ten or eleven instead of twelve, (c) unfashionable.

At 11.30 we entered the large store where we usually bought Diana's shoes. We went up in the lift which from its wall advertised the services of Mr Wart, chiropodist, and always made Diana giggle, and got out on the first floor for the children's department. This in itself was a bone of contention. At twelve Diana resented sitting with rows of restless youngsters, some of whom were quite tiny, before the dolls' house and the rocking horse in order to select her shoes. In another year she would be in the women's section but at the moment her feet were quite small and she had to suffer this indignity with which I sympathised.

We waited nearly fifteen minutes for attention and I looked at my watch anxiously not wanting to be late for Dobbie. The girl who finally came couldn't have been a day over fifteen and had bouffant hair and her slip showing and spots. I said navy blue, light-weight for the weekend for this young lady. Diana said with a tiny heel and I said no and the girl looked from one to the other of us and measured Diana's foot in its white sock and said she would show us what she had.

We waited another five minutes while a baby next to us screamed and refused to have the red shoe the assistant brought put on its fat foot. It was not to be pacified either by Mother, or Nannie in grey uniform hat and coat which was becoming a rarer and rarer sight.

Our girl came back with three shoes and sat down facing us on her little stool. Diana at once turned them over to examine the heels. One was raised a little but fortunately the shoe itself was piped in red and Diana's winter coat was navy blue with light-green trimming. I said that one's no good dear, you couldn't possibly wear a decorated shoe when you've two colours on your coat already. She insisted it didn't matter and tried the shoe on and said it was super whereas in fact she hadn't even stood up in it to see if it was comfortable. She looked at her foot with her head on one side and said of course you have to picture it with stockings. That was another battle but one I was willing to concede, having to admit to myself that times indeed had changed and that girls of twelve now wore nylon stockings albeit thirty denier.

The other two shoes were quite suitable but Diana hardly looked at them cradling the one with the heel and the red piping in her hand. It was not that she particularly liked the red she said but the actual shoe; as if I was unaware that all she saw was the inch of heel, completely blinded to the rest. I made her put the other two on. They looked very suitable, but one she said pinched her little toe and the other slipped at the heel. The girl ran her fingers over the front of the first shoe and said there seemed to be plenty of room and the other she said Diana could try in a smaller size. She disappeared to track it down while I begged Diana to walk in the one she said pinched to make sure. She hobbled a few steps with an expression of agony on her face clutching the shoe with the red piping all the while. The girl came back eventually with the smaller size of the one that slipped but that, as I had thought it would be, was too tight. We were left with the one that pinched and the red piping. Isn't there something else I said and the girl went into a trance then got up and walked away and stayed away another five minutes. I was just about to call the supervisor, who was standing importantly doing nothing except direct traffic with a green band round her bosom and a pencil in her hand, when she came back with three more shoes, one beige, one brown, and one pale blue.

I looked at my watch and said come on Diana but she still clung to the shoe with the heel, and I might have relented if it hadn't been for the red on it, and said please Mummy, tears in her blue eyes as only Diana can. I said good day firmly to the sales girl who declared she was sorry and made Diana give up the shoe and went down the escalator this time and into the street.

We battled our way along Oxford Street everyone in print dresses and no stockings like Brighton beach and I said Marshalls have a children's shoe department we could try and felt Diana's resentment oozing out of her. On the way there was a window with a stunning black cocktail dress and I said isn't that gorgeous Diana? She looked at me pityingly thinking what on earth do you want to dress up for, your days are numbered, exactly as I had thought at her age when asked to admire an outfit of my mother's.

In the window of Marshalls they had gold evening pumps with diamante buckles and Diana said aren't they super? I had to remind her we were looking for shoes to wear with her winter coat. In the department an intelligent assistant asked what we wanted then disappeared, but not too far, I could see her in the background looking pensively at boxes. She came back with just one shoe saying this seems to be the nearest, Madam. It was navy blue with a nice toe and just a fine strap and the tiniest little heel that wasn't really a heel at all but was a compromise we could both accept. Diana said it was terribly comfortable and put her head on one side to picture it with a stocking again and I asked casually how much and the superior lady explained that it was Italian, hand made and cost five pounds seventeen-and-six which was more than I paid for my own shoes which I did not grow out of in three months.

Diana knew it was too expensive and said nothing leaving me in peace to fight it out with my conscience. With the shoe in my hand I gazed blankly at the central glass table on which were a red ballet shoe, a neat white leather boot, and a slipper with Noddy on, and told myself it was quite ridiculous to pay almost six pounds for shoes for a small child to grow out of.

The alternative was further tramping, arguments, disappointments. It was only shoes, only money. I made a mental apology to Tim for being such a bad manager. I would make it up, I told myself, chopping fresh cabbage, better anyway than frozen peas, by making interesting dishes out of nothing, not falling for a new lipstick colour. We'll take these, I said. Diana said they're absolutely super. I looked at my watch. There would be just enough time to drop Diana at the Haynes' and get to the Porterhouse in time to meet Dobbie.

Clarice Haynes was either a very good mother or a very bad one. I could never quite decide. Penny was an only child and Clarice wouldn't have hesitated for a moment over navy blue shoes at five pounds seventeen-and-six. The child was dressed exclusively at the White House or Fortnums, went out to dinner as often as her parents who were in the film business, and always stayed up when they entertained at home. According to Diana she had every record under the sun, a collection of dolls from every part of the world, and was allowed to watch television as much as she liked. The end result of all this was, strangely enough, that Penny Haynes was one of the sweetest children one could wish to meet. She was smiling, friendly, self-composed without appearing in the slightest precocious. Wearing a sleeveless pink and white candy-striped dress of expensive simplicity she opened the door to us and at once embraced Diana in an enormous hug.

'I'm so glad you could come. We're going swimming straight after lunch, well not straight after because of letting it go down, and then out to tea. Hallo, Mrs Westbury, won't you come in? Mummy's on the telephone but she won't be a moment.'

It was a quarter to one but I thought it rather rude to rush off without saying hallo so followed Penelope along the corridor with the Canalettos and into the white drawing-room. Clarice Haynes was saying she had to rush now darling into the white telephone. I had seen her at parents' meetings, in winter in her full length mink, in summer Balenciaga silk, and when we'd taken and fetched the children from parties. She was exceedingly good-looking and had the kind of face, with high cheek-bones, which would look good well into old age.

'Won't you have a drink?' she said. She was dressed in navy silk with white beads. 'It's so frightfully hot.'

'I have an appointment.' I loved the irony of meeting Dobbie and no-one knowing. 'I have to go.'

She put an arm round Diana who you could see like all small girls loved Clarice because she looked and smelled divine and said, 'Don't worry about Diana. We'll deliver her about six.'

I kissed Diana and she disappeared giggling and arm in arm with Penny into her bedroom and Clarice Haynes opened the door.

Going down in the lift I thought at last, Dobbie, and wondered why I felt so nervous.

I kept telling myself it was 'only Dobbie' but as soon as I entered the Porterhouse I knew it wasn't 'only Dobbie' at all. It was something far less familiar that I was walking into. It was gloomy despite the bright light outside, and you could forget it was summer. Electric light and men in dark suits; a lot of men; business lunches, I supposed, men always went for steaks. The few women were smartly dressed but not like the Causerie, in a less obvious way. I wondered whether they were wives or girl friends. I looked round and couldn't see Dobbie. It was ten past one. I suddenly panicked in case it was the wrong place or he'd changed his mind making me look foolish.

The head waiter in maroon jacket and maroon bow tie asked could he help me, bending from the waist, ear poised to receive my confidence. I said I was meeting someone and he said was it Mr Arthur Dobson and that he had just telephoned to say he was unavoidably delayed and would I be kind enough to sit at his table and have a drink.

I regained my composure and followed him to the end of the room where two fans were whirring on the wall. He pulled out a corner table, oak with red mats and gristicks in a green vase, and I slithered in and sat on the banquette and said yes I would have a sherry. He went away snapping his fingers at the wine waiter and I looked round the room to make sure there was no-one I knew. There didn't seem to be so I took off my gloves and helped myself to a gristick to nibble and tried to relax. I assumed what I considered a very soignée air. It was meant to imply that I was in the habit of lunching *à deux* with men who were not my husband instead of meeting Martha or one of the girls for coffee and a sandwich or sharing Ryvita and Danish blue with Mrs Mac. I pretended first that I was in business, fashion buyer perhaps for a large store, although really I needed a black suit and executive glasses, or the tough cookie in charge of a model agency. Each time the door opened I came back to earth and looked anxiously for Dobbie and thought it was getting rather late and really was too bad and perhaps I should show my independence and not wait. The sherry was good and I sipped it slowly to make it last as the steaks and the Béarnaise floated by.

When Dobbie came in it was casually, loose-limbed, one hand in his pocket and grinning and my inside churned. He moved to the table beating the waiter to it and sat next to me on the banquette and said I really am sorry Liz the car broke down in Wardour Street and I had to ring the AA and get a taxi and I hope you haven't been here too long.

I said no I hadn't. They brought two menus from which Dobbie chose a T-bone and I decided on chicken marengo and oxtail soup first for both of us. They took the menus away again and I looked at Dobbie and Dobbie looked at me. I felt quite shy and the panic again, then he took my hand and held it very hard and looked right into my eyes and said hallo Liz I've been thinking about you.

Seven

I said I've been thinking about you too and still holding my hand, stroking it with his thumb, he said what have you been doing with yourself? I was about to tell him about Diana and the navy blue shoes, as I would have Tim, when I thought my God no, nor about the laundry which had so thoughtlessly decided to have its annual holiday at an inconvenient moment or Mrs Mac's Ted who was now with Frigidaire's and going slow for some incomprehensible reason. I would have chattered away about all these things at home to the old Dobbie, but here in the Porterhouse things had changed and I tried to think of conversation in keeping with my new role. Tell me about Italy, he said. That was even worse because for the life of me all I could think of was the time when Diana was sick in the hired car going up to Fiesole and the laughs we had had trying to eat spaghetti like the natives in a Trattoria in Rome; family things which came out absurdly flat unless you had actually participated. Fortunately flashing through and rejecting the hundred and one things that had happened that were foremost in my mind, I remembered the Bargello which was a favourite too with Dobbie and we got well dug in with that and della Robbia, Andrea and Luca.

The oxtail soup came and the waiter with a flick of his wrist put our napkins across our laps then poured the soup expertly from silver cups into the plates. Dobbie was telling me now about Tunis. I wished I had been there with him.

The chicken marengo was superb. I'd noticed on the menu it cost eighteen-and-six and couldn't help thinking that for that I could do chicken marengo for all of us at home instead of just one portion. Then I didn't think about it but just enjoyed it listening to Dobbie. We had wine which I wasn't used to in the middle of the day and I enjoyed that too and it made me feel deliciously drowsy and thoughts of Tim and Diana and Robin and Mrs Mac at home retreated and there was just me and Dobbie in the Porterhouse. We laughed a lot and talked of general inconsequential things and when they brought the coffee in a Cona I was amazed to discover that it was three o'clock. We were sitting very close together and I was happy. Dobbie said: 'You know Liz I still feel concerned about Tim.'

I knew what he meant and it sobered me up. I stubbed out my cigarette.

'It's awfully difficult to explain,' I said.

'But you see this makes no difference to Tim and me.'

'It would if Tim knew about it.'

'He doesn't.'

'How would you react if Tim behaved in the same way?'

It was a question I had asked myself. 'I'd murder him. Anyway he wouldn't.'

'How do you know?'

'I know Tim.'

'Perhaps he thinks he knows you?'

'Men are different. Open books. Women always leave some of the pages uncut.'

'I wouldn't trade on that.'

'Tim and I are happy.'

'That's what I thought.'

'It's not enough. I'm thirty-six. I want to share Tim's life, make a home for his children and yet experience something else. The most degrading part is the hypocrisy and caution. If he asks me what I did today I shall lie.'

'Suppose you are disappointed?'

'Are you crying off?'

'Look at me.'

I looked and felt myself desirable, animated by his expression.

'You get more beautiful.'

'Not beautiful.'

'Whatever you like; but more so.'

I knew it for myself. The age I suppose. I had lost the gaucheness of youth and felt within an intangible poise, I suppose you could call it ripeness. It was this I wanted to preserve.

'Forget about Tim,' I said. 'I absolve you from all responsibility.'

Dobbie tapped the side of his brandy glass with a knife and asked the waiter, when he came, for the bill.

Outside it was hot. Twenty years earlier we would have stretched full length on the browning grass in the park; hired a boat perhaps, Dobbie rowing.

In the street, shaded by the awning of an antique shop, we faced each other.

'Back to the flat?'

I wanted to sit somewhere cool after the food and wine.

When I hesitated he said: 'I can give you my credentials.'

I knew what he was trying to say. That I had known him a long time and that going back to his flat was not the euphemism it might appear. I was well aware that Dobbie, hadn't he been good old Dobbie for years, could be trusted. It was Liz Westbury broken out in a new place I was not so sure about.

When we got to the car I asked Dobbie if he wanted to drive and he said no, go ahead and it was strange because with Tim I would have insisted. I had been driving for years but as soon as I felt Tim at my side even looking nonchalantly out of the window or pretending to read the newspaper every vestige of judgment was gone. I drove like a novice, with apprehension, as if the instructor was at my elbow. I knew it wasn't going to be like that with Dobbie. He sat calmly relaxed, and it was a real calm, waiting for me to get on with it. I drove with ease, as I usually did, even through the afternoon traffic and parked, devoid of tension, outside the Georgian house where Dobbie lived. I thought suppose Tim comes by and sees the car but then why on earth should he. His office was in Queen Anne Street and it seemed terribly unlikely.

I had been up to Dobbie's many times of course with Tim, sometimes even alone. It had been a convenient meeting place when joining Tim in town. This time it was different. I tried to imagine I was unmarried, Catherine, anything but an ageing suburbanite with two children seeking to recapture a lost youth.

The behaviour I was contemplating, that to date even with Dobbie, was I knew that of an adolescent on the threshold of a future in which anything might happen. Mine, the real one, was already circumscribed, Tim, the children, thirty-four Hazelbank, it was unlikely now that anything further, anything dynamic that was, would come to pass. The infuriating part was that now, for the first time I felt experienced, mature enough to make my mark on a world which seemed already to have passed, or at least to be passing, me by. I did not look it but I had never felt so young.

Dobbie's flat was beautiful. At the time he moved from a block within a re-development scheme in Chelsea he had been going out with an interior decorator called Christabel who had truly done him proud. He had the top floor of the house. The two main rooms, sitting-room and bedroom, had double doors connecting them and beautiful green Wilton carpet covering the whole area. He had Georgian chairs, antique pottery figures, a serpentine-fronted Regency table; it seemed criminal that he was rarely at home to enjoy it. The rest of the accommodation consisted of guest room, with Italian urns and Georgian firescreen, a kitchen which was the last word, which he never used, and a bathroom likewise, which he did.

I sat on the green brocade settee while Dobbie made a telephone call. He spoke to a Mr Parsons and got terribly angry in a very quiet way and said it wasn't good enough and he must get through to Hamburg right away and ring him back. He hung up without saying goodbye. When he turned to me I felt for a moment as if I was the next item on the agenda.

'Men are lucky,' I said.

'Why?'

'They have the world at their fingertips.'

'Women don't do so badly these days.'

'We dabble. The great things have always been done by men.'

'What about Joan of Arc?'

'Hercules, David, Napoleon, Bismarck, Lenin, Michelangelo... So many men for one Joan of Arc.'

He sat next to me on the sofa and took the cigarette out of my hand and put it in an ashtray on the coffee table and kissed me. I wasn't prepared, thinking there'd be some sort of preamble. At first I didn't respond, thinking of Tim and that I should be at home and what was I doing here, then I began to revolve in Space and forgot about Tim, rather pushed him to the back of my mind, and I did. After about three minutes, at least I suppose it was, I didn't look at my watch, I came back to earth again and thought my God what have I started and began to get panic-stricken. It was all right though because just at that moment Dobbie released me and gave me my cigarette back and sat back and said now Liz, tell me what all this is in aid of.

You could hear the faint noise of the traffic below but other than that it was completely quiet and I realised suddenly how peaceful no children or Mrs Mac or telephone or the girls dropping in and that I was cut off, escaped, and felt tremendously at peace.

'Like Topsy,' I said, 'it just grew.'

I suppose you'd call it a kind of restlessness and it had been coming on for a long time. I noticed it first when the children began to go to school all day; at least it started then but I don't think I was properly aware of it until later, when they were able to come and go on their own and I no longer had to do the taking and fetching that had divided my day into small segments. There was still the odd chauffeuring to do; elocution and music and Guides on Tuesdays. But there was time on my hands. When Robin finished with his prep school and went away there would be even more. Looking back it seemed that at one point the day was never long enough; toddlers to be fed and bathed and changed and walked and nursed and cleared up after until you were so exhausted you lived only for bed or putting your feet up and the next they were out of the house and at school all day and Mrs Mac and the machines coped with most of the work and you were just left.

'I wonder if you know what it's like,' I said. 'Every day more or less the same. Tim goes out with the children in the morning, he drops them at school, the door closes behind them and I'm alone, free. In a way I'm glad to see them go. Mrs Mac comes but there are a hundred and one things to be seen to. I'm busy all day, my hands that is. I go out;

nothing very exciting, I look forward to the time when they'll be home. My family. I imagine how it will be; stimulating, exciting. It never is. Diana won't get on with her homework, Robin's all over the place with his great big shoes, Tim is tired. It's always a disappointment. Tim is disappointed too, I can tell. He's looking for something I don't succeed in providing. Something he's dreamed about on his way home, sitting in the traffic jams. We fail each other. The dream fades as we eat dinner making polite conversation which has nothing to do with communication. Our days remain separate; His and Hers.

'After dinner we read, watch television, talk. I always seem to be waiting for something to happen. When we go to bed I feel let down because it hasn't; perhaps tomorrow. Tomorrow the door slams after them and it begins again.'

'Why don't you get a part-time job?'

'That's what Tim says. I've had enough of offices. There's nothing else I seem capable of or want to do.'

I'd worked for an advertising company before I was married and part-time until Diana was on the way. It sounded more interesting than it was. Some of the girls in the village in a similar situation, the ones who didn't devote most afternoons to bridge for which I hadn't much patience, took up hobbies, swimming, the violin, pastimes they had abandoned in their youth. Some of them went to evening classes. I tried that but it didn't last long. It was called Creative Writing. I suppose I imagined myself a budding author. It took place in a damp and freezing institute with intense people who came straight from work and were too utterly dreary for words and produced the most infantile short stories and essays to which we all had to listen. My enthusiasm soon wore off. Learn Spanish or Italian, Tim said; it would at least be useful. I had always been hopeless at languages and didn't want to go back to the effort of past participles and adjectival clauses. I had been glad enough to escape from that at school. When the actual transition came from just feeling restless to actively thinking about Dobbie I can't remember. He seemed to have been in my mind for so long.

'A melancholy picture of marriage,' I said. 'I suppose I'm putting you off. It isn't all like that. It has its moments. Sometimes, I'm deliriously happy for weeks at a time; sometimes in the depths, nothing right. The external factors remain the same. Tim, the children. It's obviously me. Why did you never marry?'

'I've told you before, I couldn't find a girl like you.'

'No, seriously.'

'I'm being serious.'

It was nice to believe.

'Remember the old days? You and Tim and the girl with the freckles…'

'Annette.'

'Annette Armstrong. You see how old I'm getting. I used to watch you and Tim, wishing it was me with you, Tim with Annette.'

'I think I knew. Women always do. You said nothing.'

'There was so much I wanted to do. I couldn't afford to get involved. Not with "nice" girls at any rate.'

'Sometimes I wonder whether we weren't too nice.'

'Meaning?'

'I never slept with anyone but Tim. There's a new morality today; a new immorality. I shan't know what to tell Diana. I think it's confusing for them.'

'I always admire the way you've brought up Robin and Diana.'

'You do? I seem to do so badly. One applies one's knowledge but they never react according to the book. They let you down. You wonder where you've gone wrong.'

'If they grow up like their Mother, they'll be all right. You're one of the most complete people I know.'

'"As others see us". That's the last thing I'd call myself. You've no idea what Tim has to put up with.'

'Has Tim no faults?'

'It's different for men. They're out doing things. They don't have to sit at home bottling it all up.'

'Poor bottled Liz.' He kissed me.

It went on for a long time and it must have been obvious how obsessed I was with him and how I'd thought of practically nothing else for months. When we surfaced Dobbie was no longer smiling and I realised it had been a mistake to come to the flat despite Dobbie's assurances and that it was all happening too soon. With an effort I remembered there was dinner to cook at home and the Haynes bringing Diana, and Robin to be fetched from the boy he was spending the day with.

I took out my compact and looked at the wreckage and realised that it was more than could be dealt with in a tiny mirror and that I was trembling.

'I'd better tidy up.'

'Don't go, Liz.'

'We should have sat in the park.'

He was looking at me steadily so I chattered on. 'Come to dinner, nothing terribly interesting, lamb, I left it on the automatic oven, I hope it works, sometimes it gets a bit temperamental.'

He said nothing.

'Will you come?'

'I don't think I could bear to sit and look

at you all evening.'

I didn't want to let him go. 'You can't just stop coming,' I said reasonably. 'Tim would think it odd.'

'We mustn't let Tim think it odd.'

'Don't be sarcastic.'

'I didn't mean to be.'

'Dobbie.' A thought suddenly struck me.

'Liz?' I loved the way he said it.

'You don't think I'm ridiculous, throwing myself at your head?'

'Look in the mirror, Liz. No, not that little one.'

I stood up and looked in the mirror over the mantelpiece in its Regency stepped frame. There was a feminine quality in the face that looked out despite the streaked make-up, an aura of desirability, of softness, nothing to ridicule.

'I was a bit afraid, thinking of Catherine, the others... I suppose there are others.'

He stood behind me holding my shoulders. 'You're too inquisitive.'

'I hate them all.'

'So do I.'

He came home and sat on the kitchen table talking to me while I prepared dinner, waiting for Tim to come home and the Haynes with Diana. I sent him into the garden for mint for the sauce and he came back with a handful of antirrhinum leaves.

The lamb was tender and went down well

although I wasn't very hungry not being used to a midday lunch and the children were full of their outings and in good spirits.

Tim told us of a client who had paid fifty thousand pounds for a Van Gogh and I said 'men again'. Only Dobbie knew what I meant and said he might just as easily have been a woman. Tim said oh no a woman would not have been sent on a mission to the Belgian coal mines nor visited all those terribly enriching brothels. I looked quickly at the children but they were playing noughts and crosses on the tablecloth with forks.

While I cleared away and made coffee Tim and Dobbie watched the middle-weight boxing sitting forward in their chairs and saying the referee should have stopped the fight in the ninth round.

We talked a bit after that then Dobbie said he must go and Tim said why so early. I felt suddenly jealous in case it was a woman. It was only nine o'clock and I knew Dobbie never went to bed before midnight.

'A date?' Tim said voicing my thoughts. 'You already have lipstick on your collar.'

Eight

I had given a lot of thought to my feelings *vis-à-vis* Dobbie and had come to the conclusion that the excitement, the joyousness I felt about the whole affair, was engendered by the fact that in Dobbie's eyes I was still Liz Westbury whereas in Tim's I had become his wife. I wanted to assert myself somehow as an individual, to escape from the daily intimacies which created neither sympathy nor understanding. Had I been able to regain this personalisation once more for Tim, I would have thrown myself at him with the same abandon I was preparing to do with Dobbie; I loved Tim but his eyes were misted with seventeen years of matrimony; mine too, to be fair, as far as he was concerned. He knew what I did all day, occupying my proper place and concerning myself with spending and getting on behalf of him and the children, yet nothing, nothing, of what was in my mind. I couldn't tell him, and he didn't ask, of my secret dreams, fancies, yearnings; the temptations I had to conquer, doubts to overcome; he was profoundly ignorant of the emotional climate in which I spent my day. It was expected of me that I shop, cook, organise, fulfil the physical needs of my family; they would have been deeply shocked to discover anything other than complete satisfaction with these functions in mind. I had become, over the years, a wife and mother; somewhere along the line Liz Westbury, Liz Palmer that was, had disappeared; simply dissolved. In her place Mrs Timothy Westbury, nurse, housekeeper, mother, gardener, cook, seamstress, cleaner, governess, administrator, did what was expected of her. I was not naïve enough to expect a vote of thanks for every bed I made, every pie I created. The feeling I had come to rebel against was that I was expected to fulfil all my functions at the proper time and that it was taken for granted that at the said proper time all the functions, despite my own whims, hopes, dreams, thoughts, would be fulfilled. The fact that I was able to cook, sew, clean, etcetera, was guaranteed by society, implied by the fact that I was married. Nobody doubted for one moment that I *wanted* to have breakfast ready at eight, dinner at 7.30. They would have been shocked, Tim most of all, to realise that my patience, my tolerance, my propriety were not built in any more than his were. He spoke of me with affection to his friends; Liz is a wonderful wife, cook, mother. It was a mantle deposited on one at the altar. Whether it fitted or not, one was destined to wear it, muffling the thing of flesh and blood struggling to get out. With the acceptance of my wedding ring I had forfeited the right to say I have no idea how to wash a shirt and today we will have no breakfast. I was a woman in a man's world and like his desk was expected to be in my place at all times. I loved Tim and hated him for his complacency. I did not know him either. Of course in the inessential things, how he liked his bath, his eggs, his reaction to my own stupidity, the children's; not what he was in the world of men; his office staff, even the most recent acquisitions, most likely knew him better. The difference was that if Tim had decided to have an affair with another woman, I would have hated it like mad, felt completely degraded, but I would have understood that it was possible, in the nature of things. Had Tim known what was in my mind, however, concerning Dobbie, he would have been completely and utterly shattered, hurt, bewildered. My fidelity was taken for granted along with the strict adherence to the regimen I had adopted. It was different for men; so the myth went. That our desires, temptations, fantasies were identical, needed to be overcome, was not acceptable; not even true. It was different for men.

On the day after my lunch with Dobbie at the Porterhouse Mrs Mac retired to bed with water-on-the-knee. Her Ted, who telephoned with the news, said she would be out of action for at least a week.

We were all ready for our outing to Kew. I had on a white dress. I took the blue overall which had been a smock when I was pregnant down from behind the kitchen door and the gloves from the pocket and called the children in from the garden, where Diana was curled in a deck-chair with a book, and Robin swinging on one leg.

'We'll have to go to Kew another day. Mrs Mac's not coming.'

'What difference does that make?' Diana said.

'There's all the housework to do.'

'Can't we leave it?'

'There's dinner to get ready for Daddy tonight. Mrs Mac was going to prepare it, and the house is in a mess. If I'd known I could have started earlier. I can't go out for the whole day, and it's hardly worth going for less.'

'It's jolly well not fair.'

Kew was a favourite. Robin took a whole loaf of bread and we always lost him for a good hour while he fed the fish which jumped out of the pond's murky water to snatch it.

'We'll go another time,' I said.

'Will you take us swimming, then?'

'This afternoon.' I was about to ask Diana

to lend me a hand, more for the company than anything, but they disappeared into the garden.

In the cleaning cupboard the Hoover was wedged behind the hard broom and the electric polisher. I tried to get it out the lazy way, without moving the other things. It stuck half-way so I had to put it back again and start from the beginning, taking out the broom and the polisher as I should have done in the first place. When it was out, the bag of course full, I reached for the dustpan on the shelf and it came down with a shower of dust and flower petals and cigarette ends. Lazy cow, I said of Mrs Mac. She had at least washed the dusters.

I decided to start on the sitting-room. When I could be bothered I tidied up at night, shaking the cushions, Tim wouldn't have these modern foam rubber things, said they were uncomfortable and only for people sitting in adverts, not really to relax in, removing the day's newspapers and emptying the ashtrays. Last night I hadn't done so, tired after my outing, leaving it for Mrs Mac. I was sorry now. It looked comfortable and lived-in at night, sordid this morning with the sun washing over it. The chair where Dobbie had sat still bore his imprint, his cigarette stubs were in the Limoges ashtray. Looking at these manifestations of him made me want him and I wondered whether he was going to phone. Beneath the sofa cushions I found half-a-crown and a red Biro and a couple of peanuts. We hadn't had peanuts since the previous weekend when Martha and Jack and Olga had Archie and a few of the others had come in for drinks on Sunday morning. My anger at Mrs Mac increased and I wondered whether I should get somebody else. By the time I had finished tidying and dusting properly, with a wash-leather and vinegar water, and Hoovering, the dust flying up through a tiny hole in the bag, I was tired and sorry I hadn't taken off the white dress instead of just putting the overall on top, and wondered where Mrs Mac got the energy.

I pushed the Hoover into the hall and put the dustpan and dusters on the stairs and came back to the doorway to admire my work. The room looked nice, cared for. I loved it in summer when you could put roses everywhere and get that *House and Garden* look of elegance. Not that it would last long. Robin would come in and hurl himself on the sofa and put the bits of the rocket he had got out of the cereal packet on the coffee-table and Diana would shed her shoes, her latest irritating habit, and that would be that. You'd have to tidy up all over again. Housework was so negative, you never had anything to show for it; not even if you spent your entire life at it, years and years and years, keeping down the dust and the moths and the accumulation of deteriorating rubbish one seemed to collect. You didn't have one single thing at the end of it all that you could produce and say this is the sum total of my life's work, this is what I have slaved, worked my fingers to the bone for. Not that I did work my fingers to the bone, not like Mrs Mac did cleaning two homes, but I did a fair bit and often thought how futile it all was. Take the cupboards. There were four of us and summer and winter and school clothes and play clothes, weekday clothes, and weekend clothes, working clothes and relaxing clothes, not to mention special equipment for the various sports Tim and the children indulged in. They all had to be kept in order on the shelves and gone through every now and again. They got in such a mess, particularly the children's, whose things rapidly became obsolete as they grew out of them. I had fits of doing cupboards. When I'd had one they would all be freshly papered, everything in neat piles, and I'd keep going back to look at the order I had created. It lasted about two days. It was not only the children who were guilty. If I was in a hurry I tossed things quickly into my own drawers, taking and rejecting gloves and scarves and handker-chiefs. However well you did the job, in no time it needed doing again. When you considered that you'd be tidying up, sorting out, chasing the dust to eternity, like

Sisyphus and his rock it became depressing. I sympathised with Esther Glover who lived next door to Martha and made her family take their shoes off at the front door, wet or dry, greeted every caller with 'wipe your feet', and emptied every ashtray as soon as you'd dirtied it. She even kept the day's newspapers in a drawer and generally made everybody's life a misery. Our husbands worked all day. I often wondered how they would like it if, at the end of it, small demons arrived and upset every single thing they had done so that next morning they would have to start all over again. Cooking was worse, I suppose; you could spend the entire day in the kitchen preparing one meal and still in ten to fifteen minutes, after the family had sat down, it would be consumed. How would an artist like it, a painter? Some women drove their husbands mad. Martha's sister, for instance, was an excellent cook but kept asking did you like the lemon-meringue pie, John? Didn't you think the filling was nice, and what about the pastry? Until you wondered if the lemon-meringue was for her husband or her husband was for the lemon-meringue. It was the only satisfaction she had.

I decided to do the kitchen next and got the breakfast dishes into the dishwasher and cleaned the frying pan with Brillo, and the cooker, where the fat had splashed, and the tops, and put away the mats and the unused cutlery and the salt and pepper and jam jars and cereal packets. I put out the milk bottles, rinsed, and swept up and removed the crumbs from the trap at the bottom of the toaster, and thought it really was rather a nice kitchen. Robin and Diana came in and said it was sweating and could they have some elevenses and I said yes although it was not quite ten, and I went up to do the beds. When I came down there were pools of Ribena on the table and on the draining board I had shined up, and a bottle of milk and the Nesquik tin and two teaspoons. The drawers were open and there was the biscuit box on the dishwasher and silver paper on the floor and crumbs by the back door. I went to the open window and was about to shout, 'Robin, Diana, come in this instant and clear up the mess you've made.' Then I looked at them sprawled on the rug, sunbathing, and thought it's the only time, absolutely the only time when you are free and the wicked part about it is that you don't know. They say that the birth of children is the death of parents, that in bringing forth progeny you have fulfilled your biological function; we who were dying knew we were alive but those who really were flowering, Robin and Diana on the rug, had no conception of their good fortune; Diana wishing the years away until she could smother her beautiful skin in make-up, Robin setting the present at naught and thinking only in terms of when he would be grown up. Grown up and dead; or dying. They lay with their legs and arms sprawled out, abandoned, Diana with the hat she had bought in Italy over her face, unaware that they were happy. They hated their lives. Diana not being allowed to do the things she imagined she wanted to do, Robin jibbing at the certain restrictions which had to be imposed. They yearned to be old, independent, grown-up. It made you want to shake them sometimes, to scream into their ears, don't you realise, you have something to hold on to, what everybody wants. No; they longed to be old.

Dobbie had said he would telephone at ten. It was five to and I felt my stomach hollow with expectation. I cleared up the mess the children had made, killing time really, not wanting to go upstairs before he rang in case I was half-way up with the Hoover. We had been taking a picnic to Kew. It was half-ready in the basket so I thought we'd have it anyway in the garden. It would be pleasant and save making lunch. It was ten o'clock and I fiddled around with the sink which was tidy, then polished up the electric kettle and the handle of the fridge and the front of the dishwasher. It was two minutes past and I thought he's forgotten and put the cloth away. As I did the phone rang and I dived into the hall like a rocket.

'Hallo,' I said, blushing to no-one. 'You're a minute late!'

'For what?' Tim said.

Tim! I looked at the receiver in horror.

'Martha,' I said. 'I thought it was Martha. Martha said she'd ring...'

'Yes. Well never mind,' Tim said. 'Look, darling, I left a name and a telephone number on a piece of paper in the top pocket of my grey suit. Do you think you can find it?'

'Hold on.' I put the receiver down by the green bowl with the roses which needed doing again, they didn't last long, and went upstairs. Lucky I hadn't said, 'Hallo, Dobbie.' I should have to be more careful in future. I found the piece of paper and it said Maxwell Murray Tat. 3934.

'What exchange is that?' I said to Tim.

'What?'

'Tat?'

'Tate Gallery.'

'Of course.'

'All right, darling?'

'Fine, yes.'

'Must rush then. See you tonight.' He blew a kiss into the telephone. I kissed him back.

It rang immediately I replaced the receiver.

'Manor 3843.'

'You sound terribly efficient.'

'Who's that?' I wasn't being caught again.

'Dobbie. What's wrong?'

'Nothing's wrong. I just wasn't sure it was you.'

'I said ten. You were engaged.'

'I know. Tim phoned.'

'Are you all ready?'

'For what?'

'Kew Gardens.'

'We're not going. Mrs Mac isn't coming.'

'Who's Mrs Mac?'

'The daily.'

'What's she got to do with it?'

He really did not know.

'She was to do everything at home while I was out.'

'Can't you just leave it? There's no-one to do anything for if you're all out.'

It was useless explaining about beds and ironing and vegetables and things and that it was the day for the collars laundry.

'We're not going anyway. I'm taking them swimming this afternoon.'

'That will be nice. What are you doing now?'

'Hoovering. I'm just going to do the up-stairs. What are you?'

'I'm at the airport. I'm just off to Paris.'

In Dobbie's world there was no dirt, no dust, no unmade beds. I wondered whether he was alone.

'What for?'

'Business. What do you think?'

'I don't know. Women?'

He laughed. 'I do work sometimes, you know. Anyway, Liz, they seem to have lost their appeal.'

'Who?'

'All the addresses in my book.'

'What about Catherine?'

'I haven't seen her. I wish you were coming with me.'

'I thought you said it was business.'

'I'd find time for you.'

'I wish I was, too.'

'Come on then.'

He was safe. Even Dobbie knew that every hour off, let alone day or weekend, had to be planned for, domestic ties subtly unwound.

'Look, Liz. They've just announced my flight.'

He hadn't of course been serious. In three minutes I would be out of his mind walking handsomely towards the plane with his briefcase.

'When shall I see you?'

'The children go back on Wednesday. I could manage Thursday.' Over a week.

'We'll go to Brighton for the day.' What would I tell Tim? 'I'll pick you up outside Baker Street Station at 9.30. The Marylebone Road entrance. Liz?'

'Mm.'

'What are you wearing?'

I looked in the mirror. The yellow duster was hanging out of my overall pocket and I was still in my slippers. I had no make-up on, my hair was all over the place and my nose shiny. Had I been my own daily help I would have given myself the sack.

'A white dress.' It was partly true.

'I can picture you. I'll take the snapshot with me.' No wonder they fell for him like ninepins.

'Dobbie, I love you,' I said.

'What's that? The loudspeaker was going.'

'I said have a good weekend.'

'Thanks, Liz. I'll see you on Thursday; 9.30.'

He didn't care that there were six interminable days to live through. Probably hadn't even counted them.

''Bye.'

He replaced his receiver and I held on to mine staring at it as if Dobbie would reappear like the genie from the lamp. The dialling tone burped rudely and I put the receiver back in its cradle.

By the time I had finished the upstairs I was hot and cross and tired and, looking out at the sunshine, resentful, but no longer peeved at Mrs Mac. Instead I regarded her as an absolute heroine to do all that tedious work every single day of the week and resolved not to carp at her any more even if she did skip the odd corner.

The white dress was dusty at the hem where the overall didn't cover it and I felt dusty all over. I undressed and took a shower, not bothering to clean it, I'd done it once, so really I might not have troubled, and put on a beach dress I had worn in Italy and gold-thonged sandals. I felt cool and comfortable and better, and brushed my hair off my face and decided I really looked quite young and put on pink lipstick and sun-filter cream and just a little mascara and went down to prepare the rest of the picnic and do the vegetables and make some sort of dessert for the evening.

At 12.30 when I took out the picnic basket the children were still motionless on the rug. I though they'll get sunstroke and then no they wouldn't because children never did get any of the things you always said they would, like colds when they got their feet wet and didn't change their socks or tummy-aches from eating oranges and milk.

They sat up reluctantly then bustled about when they saw the picnic basket and they were brown from Italy and really nice-looking kids and I suddenly felt lucky and happy and at peace and at their disposal like the calm and contented mothers in the family magazines.

Nine

The mood lasted all through lunch during which we played Twenty Questions, and Knock-Knock Who's there? Taking me back to my own childhood, although Robin and Diana swore they had invented it, and Geography Endings at which they beat me.

They helped me clear away and got their swimming things without any fuss, Diana not even having to turn the house upside down for her cap. We had the roof off the car and switched on the radio and sang to the music all the way to the pool.

I didn't go in to help them undress. I hated the disinfectant smell of the changing-rooms and the soggy floors and the laundry boxes you had to put your clothes in, and exchanged for a numbered disc to pin to your swimsuit, and the middle-aged women attendants defeated by life calling 'come along now dear' to someone every minute of the day.

Outside by the pool it was hot and sunny, people lying around on towels and laughing and diving and kids screaming and you could believe you were on the Continent because of the sun. I put on my dark glasses and sat down on the grass verge near the kiddies' pool, where the tiny tots were paddling on fat legs, and listened to other Mums shouting at their children and from my serenity pitied them.

Robin and Diana came out in their swimsuits and gave me their watches to keep and their towels and I helped Diana with her cap which was always difficult to get on over her long hair and they were away threatening to push each other into the water.

It was more restful than Kew really. I suppose everything has its compensations, and it wasn't at all unpleasant just relaxing in the sun instead of trailing through the hot-houses gazing at bananas and giant water-lilies and thinking you couldn't survive another moment. I wasn't worried about the children in the pool because they were both good swimmers. I had taken them both through two miserable winters every Tuesday night after school in the dark to the Municipal baths where with scarlet floats round their arms they had progressed from clinging tearfully to the side of the bath to swimming like little fishes in the deep end. Stretching my legs in front of me, I hadn't repainted my toe-nails since Italy and they needed doing, I leaned back on my hands and put my face up to the sun which made everything look so different. In its embrace I felt like Lollabrigida and Bardot and Loren, and wished Dobbie were there to see me, and capable of anything. Dobbie not Tim; I was afraid Tim would shatter the moment by saying teatime or I wouldn't say no to a drink. He liked to eat and drink on time while I could let hours go by not caring or eat at any time according to my mood. Of course it wasn't Tim's fault and dated, I knew, from his prisoner-of-war days when there just wasn't anything to eat except some thin soup and rice if they were lucky and they'd sit and think of all the eating and drinking they were going to do when they came home. Often when I watched him carving the roast on Sundays I'd think of him in his P.O.W. clothes, weighing six stone as he had when they released him, and standing behind barbed wire, dreaming of this moment. I often wondered if he appreciated it now that it was here, thanked God every time he sat down to a meal. When I asked him he said he couldn't live in the past and he hardly ever thought about those days, they were bad enough at the time, and he had no desire to relive them. I often thought about them though and tried to put myself behind the barbed wire in the abysmal conditions with not enough to eat. Try as I would I simply could not feel anything, any more than Tim could feel what it was like having a baby from my inadequate description. It wasn't only Tim, I knew, but thousands and thousands of others who had suffered even worse privations. It didn't help when Tim explained that there was no sum total of human suffering but each man could only suffer so much for himself and that was the limit of human endurance. I thought you must remember the past, hang on to it so that you didn't make the same mistake again. Tim said no, you must go forward; in the future lay hope.

I felt my nose burning and opened my eyes to get the sun-filter cream from my bag. There was a man sitting on the wall in swimming trunks, beautifully muscular and tanned, with a gold chain round his neck, and black glasses. He was looking in my direction and I thought that would be funny picked up at the local swimming pool, me, then I noticed he wasn't looking at me exactly but at my left ear and I turned round and just behind me there was an au-pair so brown she was almost black, with one of those inflated figures swelling scornfully out of an inadequate black bikini. I found the cream and spread it slowly over my face feeling matronly and that I had never at any time looked like that, not even at seventeen. I looked again to make quite sure he wasn't staring at me and of course he wasn't. I was another Mum looking after children in the pool; a depersonalised fragment of the crowd. I took another glance at the girl and saw that her hair was long and wet and guessed that she had swum the pool like a mermaid, hair floating, scornful of caps and keeping your set dry and other such mundane matters that complicated my life.

I shaded my eyes. Robin and Diana were fighting in the pool, beneath the diving-boards, and I shouted 'Robin; Diana!' anxiously, hysterically, like all the others. Jennifer! Hilary! Come here! Tell Peter! Come out this minute! They didn't hear me. It wasn't surprising with the noise of the water and the screaming. They were struggling together like little porpoises. I think Robin was trying to take Diana's swimming cap off. I went to the edge of the pool and waved and Robin seeing me waved back, one hand still grabbing Diana, and I signalled that I wanted them to come out and went back to where I had left my bag.

They came dripping, panting like puppies. I pushed at their legs saying careful you're making me all wet. Robin's nose was running and I told him and he wiped it with the back of his hand. They stood there shivering and said what do you want? I said I won't have this horse-play, it's dangerous, if you want to swim, swim, but leave each other alone. Diana said Robin started it, he wanted my cap. Robin said, liar, you tried to pull me under. They both said I didn't and

I said if there's any more argument you can come out and get dressed, listening to myself being angry. They looked at each other and went back to the pool and I moved away from the puddle they had left on the grass. I knew that they had only been playing and that they weren't really in any danger. The thing would have worked itself out. I was unable to prevent myself though from making the conventional response, from hauling them out of the water and giving them a telling-off the general lines of which were so familiar to all of us I doubt if they even heard. They just waited until it was over so that they could get back into the pool. In ten minutes they were back, hungry and holding their hands out for money for the snack-bar.

'You've only just had lunch,' I said.

Robin held his stomach and rolled his eyes. 'I'm starving.'

'So am I,' Diana said.

'Pass my bag, then.'

He opened it and looked in, dripping all over the contents.

'I said pass it.'

'I was looking for your purse.'

'No-one told you to look for it. I do wish you'd listen. What do you want?'

'Coca-Cola and a Bandit and a lolly and a packet of crisps.'

'Me too.'

'That's far too much.'

'I'm starving.'

'So am I.'

I took out a two-shilling piece and gave it to Diana. 'You can have this between you.'

'You can't get hardly anything,' Diana said.

'Well it's not tea-time and you've only just had lunch.'

'Make it half a dollar,' Robin said.

'If you're going to argue you can't have anything at all.'

They went off towards the snack-bar, jog-trotting. The man with the chain round his neck was looking at me now. I suppose he was enjoying the hackneyed little scene. I was wrong, I knew. I had made no attempt to put myself in their situation, hungry from the pool. Once again, from Olympian heights, I had treated them as children. Children they were but people too. One forgot too often. It was easier to forget. I was not alone. It should be called having 'people' really, not having children at all. Perhaps then one would be more prepared. It would not come with so much of a shock, the realisation that they had minds, thoughts, feelings of their own; one would not pigeon-hole their little doings into lumpish categories. Having a baby sounded cute; a bundle wrapped in a blanket. Having a person implied something more serious. Should we not reflect more? Two, three, or four extra persons round the house each with a personality to be cultivated was an undertaking, needed consideration. We did not consider. We had them, babies, and ignored their demands, not to be fed and clothed, but to be treated as human beings with equal rights, as long as possible. We presupposed a love and affection that we imagined came built-in with the relationship; were surprised to discover it was not implicit. True, mothers had their maternal instinct, if there was such a thing, to help them. With fathers it came more hard. Before the war, if fathers were wealthy they kept their offspring insulated in the nursery; at the other end of the scale they saw equally little of them, coming home only to sleep. The cataclysm, which had swept away Nannies and nurse-maids, save for the few extant in Kensington Gardens, had thrown up a new father-child relationship. Their company was forced upon each other. It was good to see them together in the parks on a Sunday morning or en-grossed in the finer points of the working of an electric railway. The ramifications spread wider, however, than that.

When Robin and Diana were young, at the crawling stage or toddling, Tim had played with them, given them rides on his shoulders, bathed them on many occasions, helped me put them to bed. He was a good father. He liked talking to Robin, man talk, to Diana about her school-work, current affairs which she didn't seem able to grasp, busy with her idols. The trouble was that now when he had finished with them they could no longer be tucked up tidily in bed. They hung around. You had company when you wished to be quiet. They had their own rooms, record players, desks, armchairs, everything, but when Tim came home they wanted to be with him. Sometimes the sight of Diana slopping around, no shoes, face plastered with theatrical make-up, drove him to distraction. I defended them, pleading they were people, individuals in their own rights. I knew I was just as bad.

My earlier mood of well-being had vanished. The ground was hard but there was nothing to sit on. I was fed up with the pool and wished I was back in the garden where I had a siesta chair which supported your legs and gave you the impression you were floating, suspended comfortably, in mid-air.

The children came back, sucking Coca-Cola through straws, and a packet of crisps each and a penny change. I said shall we go and they looked horrified and said we've only just come and I knew I was there for what remained of the afternoon.

By the time we got home it was five o'clock. Olga had turned up with Rosanna who at thirteen was a little stunner, and with her hair done up in a dough-nut and developing figure and South-of-France bikini looked years older than Diana instead of six months. We had spent the afternoon gossiping while the children swam. Olga told me amongst other things that Dick Howland, whom we all knew, had run off with a divorcée who ran a boutique in Sloane Street, and left poor Margery with three children and another on the way. It was interesting because the legend that went with the Howlands was that they were one big happy family and they always seemed to be enjoying themselves *en masse* and Dick and Margery never dumped the children on to grandparents and went away or anything like that.

When I'd unlocked the front door Robin and Diana streaked through into the garden to put themselves under the hose, as if they hadn't had enough water for one day, and dumped the bag with the wet swimming things on the hall carpet. I picked it up and sorted out the things, putting the towels into the machine for the morning, rinsing out the costumes and Diana's hat and putting the bag into the cupboard. Listening to the screams from under the hose I put the kettle on, had a wash while it boiled, and came down to make a cup of coffee and start on dinner.

I was standing over the cooker when Tim

147

arrived. He put his arms round me and kissed the back of my neck and smelled hot and of the City.

'It's certainly been a scorcher,' he said, loosening his tie and taking his coat off. 'What did you do?'

'Took the kids swimming.'

'Lucky. Did you go in?'

'No.'

'Why not?'

I didn't know. I liked swimming well enough in the Mediterranean, on holiday, although it was a thing I didn't do particularly well. I wouldn't dream of taking off my things and joining the children in the local pool. The mothers sat by and watched by tradition.

'I just didn't.'

'You'd have been the belle of the pool.'

He meant it. I thought of the girl in the black bikini. I should have been glad that Tim still thought me as attractive as when we had met. Perversely I wasn't.

'I'm going to shower.' He said that every hot night.

Then I'll have a drink.

'Then I'll have a drink.'

He lifted the lid of the saucepan.

'It's only potatoes.'

'I love you. Get the ice out, honey.'

How many women had husbands who loved them after seventeen years? I tried to make it mean something, to let it envelop me. It did nothing to fill the need that was inside me. Need for what? For Dobbie? I opened the great fridge with the light that went on inside, not knowing.

'Pity about Kew,' Tim said over the fried veal. 'You'll have to go another day.'

'Go back to school next week,' Robin said. 'What have you been doing with yourselves all day?'

'Nothing,' Diana said smartly.

'Mummy took you to the pool.'

'Yes.'

'Well, that's not nothing.'

'Mummy already told you we went to the pool.'

'It's still not nothing.'

'I didn't say it was. You knew, though.'

'Sociable lot,' Tim said.

I could see he was getting irritated. 'Bring some bread,' I said to Diana. 'I forgot to put it on the table.'

She got up. She had changed into a blue cotton skirt and T-shirt and looked fresh and pretty.

'Where are your shoes?' Tim said.

'Oh Daddy!'

'How many times have I told you?'

She walked towards the kitchen.

'Put them on!' Tim bellowed.

'Tim!'

Diana came back and felt under the table,

149

looking sulky.

'It's too hot for shoes.'

'Don't argue. It only takes a moment to get something in your foot.'

She sat down.

'Your mother asked you to get the bread.'

Diana rolled her eyes. 'Oh glory!' She got up.

'And don't be impertinent!'

She made a face at Robin on the way to the door to save her own.

We were left with the fried veal which was nice but which I knew Tim was not now enjoying, and an atmosphere. Tim had not meant to upset Diana any more than Diana had intended to be rude to her father. It was always the way though. They couldn't be together for more than a few minutes without rubbing each other up the wrong way. It was laughable when you thought what enlightened parents we had made up our minds to be.

Diana came back with the bread which no-one wanted and sat down sulkily and Tim put down his knife and fork half-way through the veal and said it was too hot and that made me cross because it was hotter still cooking it and that left just Robin unperturbed in the private world of his own he always lived in.

Tim told me why he had wanted Maxwell Murray's telephone number. A big deal was about to go through but at the moment it was all terribly hush-hush. It seemed aeons ago since the morning when I had given the number to him thinking it was Dobbie on the phone and I didn't really understand what was supposed to be going on anyway.

When we'd finished and cleared away we settled in the sitting-room with the French windows open on to the garden which was getting brown from lack of rain and which Tim said he was going to water.

Diana was sprawled out on the floor with the *Daily Express,* reading the Gambols which was about all she ever read of the newspaper, and Robin was glued to the *TV Times* to see what was on.

'Did you hear about Margery Howland?' Tim said. 'Dick's pushed off and left her with three kids and one in the oven.'

'Yes. Olga told me.'

'We always quote them. Happy family and all that.'

'You can never tell,' I said.

'People's marriages seem to be breaking up right and left. Look at the ones we know married about the same time as us.'

'It must be the dangerous age,' I laughed.

'I thought it was seven years, the itch, not seventeen.'

'Have you had many itches?'

Tim laughed. 'The odd moment. Don't we all?'

He picked up the two evening papers he always brought in with him and handed me one.

I read the headline, a split in the Labour Party, they were always having splits, then turned to the 'Diary'. There had been a party on somebody's yacht with a list of 'names' a yard long and peaches flown in from California. Half London's population was in Scotland and the other half had been at the River Room last night where the theme of Lord Mitcham's twenty-first birthday fancy-dress party had been *Midsummer Night's Dream*. The Lord Chancellor had gone as Bottom and the Honourable Miss Lavinia (Boo) Graham as Hermia and the American ambassador's wife as Titania. Everyone had had caviare and sole véronique and pheasant from his lordship's estate and an absolutely fabulous time while I had been sitting in the morning room with Tim, after Dobbie had gone, watching a poor instalment of *The Avengers* and putting a patch in Robin's trousers.

Ten

It seemed that Thursday was never going to come. On Wednesday with a hallelujah of relief I got the children back to school not minding for once the pre-breakfast trauma nor clearing in their wake the trail of holiday clutter they left behind. Mrs Mac was back with a bandage round her knee and full of grumbles but coping and I did the morning chores then went off to the hairdresser's to get my hair done for Dobbie.

I knew most of the women in the hairdresser's. It was a pretty regular clientèle and quite a fashion parade, stunning little dresses or suits, and lovely legs in lovely stockings, and gorgeous handbags and sun-glasses and poodles. Many of them had just come back from somewhere and others were just off or even the same ones having their hair done in between. Martin and Jack and Stanley who lived in Ealing or Blackheath or Notting Hill back-combed with all their might and main, turning heads into golliwogs before smoothing them to elegance, and squirted clouds of lacquer and listened to tales of Majorca, Malta and Torremolinos. It was quite a club and some members attended every day to have their hair dressed. Lately they were tripping in with wigs in boxes to be cleaned and styled while their own hair was lifted and bleached and rinsed and tinted and anointed with everything from beer to eggs. Husbands thought that all you did in the hairdresser's was to have it washed and set. It may have been like that once but now it was big business, an industry. Every other shop seemed to be a hairdressing salon with identical blown-up Italian pictures outside and pale green heads in the window and its selection of Mervins and Antoines and Pauls rolling away like mad. They were assisted by the Sandras and Brendas and Shirleys ranging from the genuinely pleasant to the downright petulant, gazing into space, and pondering on new shoes with pointed toes, their hands deep in lather. Heads waiting patiently over basins, blued or blacked, walked out two shades of mink or amber. My own hair was dark brown; a not bad colour with the odd grey hair here and there. I'd always determined not to go in for tinting. Apart from being expensive to keep up it took ages and once you were on the merry-go-round it was difficult to get off. I'd had flu though two years ago and when I recovered felt hideous. My face had got thin and my hair dull and Martin said why not a colour, it just needs a little lift? I needed more than that. I said all right just a rinse then to see. He said a rinse wouldn't do anything to your hair it's too dark. We'd have to give it an oil bleach first then a tint. I hummed and hahed and looked round the salon and everyone seemed to be going one colour or another and I felt stodgy and said all right. I went through agonies while they plastered it with white stuff, which prickled my scalp, then put me under the steamer, where I steamed, then gave me books to read and I thought they'd forgotten about me. They hadn't though and kept coming back to look and mutter and dry bits off. When I thought it was all over, I'd already been an hour and a half, it was time for the tint and I had to wait for that too. I thought my God what am I doing, but it was too late, and I submitted to the shampoo and set feeling as if I had been there for years. When I got home I was brightish red although I'd agreed to auburn but Martin said it was difficult to judge the first time. He could tone it down next week if I didn't like it; more money. Tim said it was lovely, good old Tim, and I varied between hating myself for looking cheap and loving the new me on a good day. It didn't end there though because the roots grew dark and looked dreadful and every week or so it was more bleach and tint and time and money and I understood where the platinum blondes in the *Tatler* who always looked so fabulous at St Moritz or Nassau spent their days. I decided that the upkeep was too much and that I would grow it out and go back to my natural colour. It took me a year and when it was back I hated it but was determined not to get involved again. I didn't until Tim's annual accountants' ball and I had a new white dress and wanted to look stunning and in a weak moment allowed Martin to start all over again. I wasn't red now but a kind of warm brown. That, I supposed, was how I was going to remain, with my touchings-up and ash-rinses when it went yellow and tints when it got too red. Like all the others, I was committed. Now, I said, I want it to look really good. Martin, steel comb poised, in shirt sleeves, tight trousers, and winkle-pickers with elevators on the heels, said 'Going somewhere nice?' and I said yes, knowing he imagined a party, not a day in Brighton with my query lover.

I watched him like a hawk and knew by the way he put the rollers in and was paying attention that it would look all right. I relaxed under the drier enjoying the freedom and the children being back at school and read about the dance in aid of Handicapped Children where everyone seemed to have stepped straight from Dior, and the Hunt Ball where they had never heard of him, and copied out a recipe for salmon mousse. He took a long time combing me out, impervious to the glares of the others waiting to be combed out or with wet heads. When he stepped back with the mirror I knew it was OK even if I did have to sleep on my nose.

The difficulty was Tim. It would have been easier to be honest. There was no reason why I shouldn't go to Brighton for the day with Dobbie but on the other hand there was no earthly reason why I should. I decided against the truth. Most of the shops have their autumn things in, I said, I shall be out all day, I'm going to look for a suit. In this weather, Tim said. Oh yes, there's no point in waiting until it gets cold and everybody rushes. I'd rather go while there's a selection. It was the evening that was going to be difficult. I doubted whether we should be back by four when I usually got back for the children. I gave Robin the key although Tim didn't like me doing it, in case I was a bit late, and left everything ready for dinner, a casserole in the automatic oven and the rest to chance.

In the morning I'd looked at Tim un-suspecting in his lightweight suit and he'd said have a good day and kissed me. I loved him more than ever and knew that he must never find out and hurried them all out of the house and got ready for Brighton.

It was ages since I'd been on a tube train, going everywhere by car. I felt that I didn't belong and that everyone was looking at me but I suppose I was just excited. My heel got caught in the escalator and the wind hurtling down the corridors blew my beautiful hair out of place and I was sure brought smuts with it. I went to the Ladies at Baker Street to tidy up. I smiled at myself in the tiny mirror of my compact and then went up the steps in my light dress, my coat over my arm, to meet Dobbie.

He was waiting at the top of the steps in his green Mercedes. For one moment I thought of Tim at the office and the children and that I was behaving like a tart, Brighton and all that, then Dobbie leaned over and opened the door and took my coat and said hallo Liz and I thought don't be ridiculous.

It was nice to be in a sports car. It was the sort of thing Tim and I had always wanted but of course with children to put in the back and luggage at holiday times it was quite impractical. Housewives' Choice was on the radio and I was usually pottering around at home instead of stopping and starting in the traffic, the streets chock-a-block with cars and taxis and lorries and buses. We didn't say much listening to the music for Mrs Jones of Sidcup and Maureen and Arthur in the Isle of Wight and Mrs Hathaway in hospital in Dorking. Acutely aware of Dobbie next to me, I put back the clock, dreaming I was single again, that anything was possible. It was surprising how easy it was, momentarily at any rate, to set so many years, so much, at nought.

At Haywards Heath we stopped and took the roof off and I was glad I'd remembered a scarf to tie round my head. Dobbie looked at me with approval and kissed me and I felt terribly happy and the mood prevailed all the way to Brighton.

We parked outside the Metropole between a maroon Rolls and a black and went in for coffee. Had I been with Tim and the kids it would have been straight to the beach and elevenses on the pebbles. Coffee in a silver pot out on the terrace seemed terribly civilised.

'Where's your next trip?' I asked Dobbie, really wanting to know when.

'Russia, the end of the next week, via Prague and Warsaw. I dislike Russia. From the plumbing up it's depressing.'

'I'd like to go; jump out of my rut.'

'You've just been to Italy.'

'We went last year. I'd like to go somewhere different, San Francisco, Japan, somewhere really far away.'

Dobbie stubbed out his cigarette. 'Wasn't it Proust who said it's better to see one place with a hundred eyes than a hundred difference places with one pair of eyes?'

'I wouldn't know.' I wouldn't. I had stayed on into the sixth form at school but hadn't been bright enough for Higher Schools as we called it then. I had been introduced to Proust but had stuck fast a third of the way through Volume I of *Remembrance of Things Past,* finding Swann an incalculable bore and knowing I would never get any further. Dobbie was very well up in that sort of thing. He could talk plays and literature with anyone although he had never had any higher education, going straight into business. He dabbled in Philosophy and spoke fluent French and German and Italian and read Racine in the original.

'Proust is out of my depth,' I said, shutting my eyes against the sun. 'Like Existentialism. I can never remember what it means.'

'It's a protest,' Dobbie said, 'against the view that human beings are the hapless playthings of historical forces. A justification of the freedom and importance of the human personality. We are all, in other words, free.'

'To do what?'

'To choose. Our future is not altogether predictable.'

Mine seemed to be mapped out. The gayness of the beginning of married life and the importance of maternity had faded. As a young girl there had always been something new; now there was Dobbie. I looked at him filling the cane chair yet not immobile, poised as if ready for flight to one of his faraway places. I knew that Tim, if he was pushed, could manage very well without me, the children would always be more or less ungrateful. I wanted to be wanted.

Dobbie paid for the coffee and we left the car because we were coming back to the hotel for lunch and walked, free on a Thursday, towards the stony beach. We stumbled hand in hand over the pebbles and the men in braces with knotted handkerchiefs over their balding heads. Near a breakwater which was quiet we stopped and Dobbie lay back on the stones. I lay beside him with my head on his shoulder and wondered what would happen if somebody came by who knew me.

'Are you going to sleep with me?' Dobbie said.

It took me by surprise.

'Yes.'

'When?'

'I don't know. There are certain mental hurdles to be overcome. You forget I've been a faithful wife for seventeen years.'

He put a hand on my breast. 'We could stay at the Metropole.'

'I'd rather you didn't rush me.'

'You shouldn't be so desirable.'

'Am I?'

'Doesn't Tim tell you?'

'Yes he does.' He knew me too well, loved me too well. With Dobbie I would be free.

'You don't love him then?'

161

'I do; yes.'

He waited.

'It's not Tim and I, Dobbie, it's marriage. It's not the best medium for love.'

'You'd do away with it, then?'

'I didn't say that. There are great delights; besides, what about children?'

'According to some, child-bearing is merely a purposeless and unjustifiable increase in the world's population.'

'Don't you wish you had children?'

'Occasionally. I'm too selfish. They take too much.'

'I always wanted six. After Robin I realised it wasn't children I wanted as much as to be with child. I keep getting great fat longings to be pregnant; to feel the wonderful, satisfying warmth of it. Of course you can't just keep on.'

'If I were married to you I would want a child.'

'If you were married to me we wouldn't be lying here. You'd be away and probably glad and I'd be at home washing your socks.'

'What makes you think that things are going to be different with me?'

'I am choosing you. There is no conqueror, no conquered.'

'You chose Tim.'

'In the beginning, yes. In the beginning things were all right. I don't choose him afresh each time we make love though if we were free I probably would. It's a silent rebellion.'

'Against what?'

'Two people shut up in a box with man as master.'

'It sounds Victorian.'

'It hasn't changed. We drive cars, go out to work, sit on committees but it's still the man who pays the piper, calls the tune.'

'Someone has to.'

'Do they? I think it leads to a cold war fought nightly beneath a million ceilings. We are not naturally perverse. You force us to be.'

'One wouldn't know, looking at you; you and Tim.'

'I didn't say we weren't happy. I feel I have an infinite and untapped capacity for love.'

'Prove it.' His eyes were over mine.

'Are you angry, because I'm dallying?'

'You can dally as long as you like; provided it's not too long.'

I was aware at that moment that I had everything; a husband who loved me and whom I loved; two very good children, a lover with whom I was as yet innocent at my command.

I was surprised when Dobbie said it was time we went back for lunch. Absorbed with him I had been unaware of the general exodus around us. Our bank of pebbles was deserted. He stood up, back to the sea and sun, and held out his hand to pull me up. I stumbled on the stones and was in his arms, wishing my mind was as deserted as the shore, empty of Hazelbank and all it represented.

We wandered back to the hotel like lovers and I went to the ladies' room to wash. With horror I looked at myself reflected in the peach-glass mirror and doubted my ability to convince Tim I'd achieved my sunburned nose in Knightsbridge. I applied make-up which took off some of the shine and thought it looked not too bad.

Dobbie was in the bar, sherry and black olives waiting, and said where have you been?

'Trying to do something about my nose.'

'It looks all right to me.'

'Tim will wonder where I caught the sun.'

Dobbie offered the olives and I thought Tim's favourites then don't be a bore Dobbie doesn't want to be constantly reminded of Tim. I noticed the women, the young ones particularly, looking twice at Dobbie and curiously at me.

'You must have a fabulous time abroad,' I said.

'In what way?'

'Women.'

'I work sometimes.'

'Not in the evenings.'

'It's often quite dreary in the evenings;

particularly the Iron Curtain countries; feather beds and mushrooms on the bathroom ceilings.'

'No beautiful comrade?'

'None.'

'My heart bleeds. What about Catherine?'

'What about her?'

'She's very beautiful.' I felt depressed. He refused to be drawn.

'What age do you like them best?'

'Your age.'

'No seriously.'

'I am being serious.'

I sighed knowing I would never know and agreed with Dobbie that we should eat.

After lunch we sat on the terrace and I remembered I hadn't telephoned Tim.

'Why do you have to ring him?' Dobbie said from behind his black glasses.

'I always do, or he rings me if I'm at home.'

'That's nice.'

'We always have done.'

'Any luck, darling?' Tim said.

'With what?'

'The suit.'

'No. Not yet, that is. You were probably right, it is a little too early.'

'Never mind. I'm glad you phoned. Look, Liz. Burrington and Charlton-Jones have just flown in from New York about this merger and I want them to get together with

Maxwell Murray. I think I shall have to dine them tonight.'

I looked at the receiver.

'Sorry, darling,' Tim said. 'They just called me from the airport.'

I was trying to work things out.

'Why don't you ring up Mrs Lockhart to sit, and go to a film with Martha and Jack, Thursday's their night, isn't it?'

'Yes,' I said. 'Yes, they usually go on Thursdays.'

'Sorry, but it can't be helped.'

'Don't worry.'

'I hope you find your suit.'

'I'm sure I shall.'

'Don't overdo it.'

'No.'

'See you tonight then, darling.'

'Yes.'

I had the rest of the day for Dobbie. I told him and he took my hand.

'You aren't fed up with me?' I asked.

'You know you're my girl; you always have been.'

'I wonder what would happen if your bluff was called.'

'Sit down and have your coffee.'

'In a moment.'

'Where to now?'

'I have to phone Mrs Lockhart.'

Eleven

That was September and it was now November. Four months had passed between the thought and the deed.

By the end of the day that had started at Baker Street Station and ended at the Four Hundred via Brighton I felt stimulated, live and young again as I hadn't done for years. At the Four Hundred we saw one of our leading film stars with her hair a foot high and elfin face smudged with enormous eyes. You could well believe the tales that her toilette took her two and a half hours to complete. Her companion, screen and life, wore make-up too, giving him a bronze glow which owed nothing to the great outdoors, and paid court with much flashing of inch-square golden cuff-links. For an entire day I hadn't cooked or thought of meals, chased dirt, except on my face, or admonished the children. I gave myself over to Dobbie who said what we were to do, smoothed every path, and anticipated my needs with solicitude.

It was perhaps a mistake to go up to his flat after Brighton but at the time I did not really think. My dress wasn't suitable for the evening. I should have gone home to change but Dobbie said it would do. It was after all still summer and you could just get away with print.

While Dobbie showered I roamed round his bedroom with its snow leopard rug and French patterned wallpaper. He had opened his cupboard to get his fresh shirt and left it open and he must have had at least four dozen shirts all terribly tidy and new-looking from Sulka's. The ties were neat too, each one neatly rolled. I imagined him doing them meticulously before he went to bed, putting his shoes in trees, there was a pair under the chair, trees in his slippers too. His suits, all weights, hung regimented, shoulder to shoulder, as if he had a valet to care. I thought what an absolute blessing he'd be to any wife.

The bed was covered with purple linen piped with white and a white bed-head against a blue wall. I sat on it wallowing in the luxury, not of Dobbie's flat but of having a lover, in name at any rate. I enjoyed a feeling of opulence as if Liz Westbury had taken on a new existence outside her ordinary self.

I could hear him splashing about in the shower and lay back against the white cushion, drowsy after the Brighton sun, and thought with detachment what if this was my wedding night, comparing it with the other.

The detachment was significant. Regarding my relationship with Dobbie I felt omniscient, clear-sighted, and mistress of myself. With Tim I had been confused, love and sentiment and physical desire undistinguishable one from the other. I was no longer a girl and felt myself to be unshockable, no modesty to defend.

Alone with Tim on the first night of our honeymoon in Cornwall I had been bewildered by fatigue, engendered by the wedding and its foregoing hectic weeks, by a certain shyness brought about by anticipation of the unknown, by a host of fleeting and conflicting requirements. They had to do, at the same time, with the wish to be respected and violated, ravaged with no loss of dignity, subjugated yet preserved. I had closed my eyes and given myself to Tim. I was fortunate in my choice of husband. He knew what he was doing; I did not. If we pleased each other it was by chance, instinct perhaps. With Dobbie I would be in complete command of my senses, allowing them freedom or pulling on the reins at will. My relationship with Tim as far as sex was concerned had not been unsuccessful; from my new standpoint, the years making me what I was, I wanted to try another.

Looking at the ceiling, the faintest wash of blue, I was surprised at my own unmuddled thinking; aware of a feeling of joyous excitement in the knowledge that Dobbie was within splashing distance and the ennui of my normal routine both out of sight and almost out of mind. I knew it was an evasion, that this was not my life, but I aided and abetted myself in the deception that I was master of my fate and capable of anything.

With how many women, I wondered, had Dobbie made love on this bed? I pictured them afterwards, smoking, Dobbie with his lazy eyes. How would I measure up, beyond my prime, with the young ones, the Catherines; did they know what it was all about? And what of Dobbie? Gentle, tender, clumsy, brutal, rapacious? One could not always go by looks.

He came out of the shower in a white bath-robe, rubbing the back of his neck with a towel, and smelling of soap and aftershave. I sat up, relinquishing with reluctance my day-dream, and he sat down beside me. I had things to say but I didn't say them because I was in his arms and rolling over and thinking nice and what the hell then no not now I wasn't ready. I pulled away and stood up and he lit a cigarette and I laughed because I'd thought of him doing that afterwards and he said:

'What's funny?'

'Nothing.'

'You aren't by any chance leading me up the garden?'

I shook my head not laughing any more.

'What are we waiting for then?'

I couldn't explain that it was my up-bringing getting in the way. It seemed so horribly crude to fall into bed with Dobbie without a suitable period of courtship although there was nothing to court and I'd known him all my life.

'Sorry to be difficult.'

'I didn't mean to rush you. You looked lovely there on the bed.'

'You know what's so nice,' I said. 'We know none of the irritating things about each other. I don't know if you leave puddles in the bathroom, your dirty socks on the floor, you don't know what I'm like first thing in the morning.'

He fastened his watch, the cigarette in his mouth.

'Does it matter?'

He meant it. His world was different to mine.

'Yes, it does.'

I picked up my handbag.

'Where are you going?'

'To find out about the puddles.'

When I came back, I felt refreshed. I'd found Numero Cinq toilet water on the white shelf against the black-painted wall and promised myself not to ask whose it was. Dobbie was dressed in a dark suit. He was looking out of the window.

'Sure you want to go out?'

'Sure.'

He put his arms round me. 'Don't make it too long.'

He didn't know how close I was, touched by his tenderness, to making it then.

We danced all night. Until 11.30 at any rate. At the next table was a party of four; a Spanish woman, older than I, very beautiful, terribly gay, with a Don Juan of a husband, six foot tall and grey moustached, two handsome, elegant sons. They danced, the sons with the mother, kissing her when they escorted her back, the husband cheek-to-cheek with his vivacious wife. They drank champagne. At eleven o'clock the father handed over some money to the eldest son, and the boys, laughing, confident in their elegant looks, suits, kissed the mother on both cheeks and left. Alone with their father, the woman, hair drawn back from fine, olive cheekbones, was no less loving, gay.

The charade depressed me.

'What's the matter, Liz?' Dobbie said.

I smiled. 'Nothing.' I could not have explained even to myself.

We danced.

There were elderly men with pert, shiny little girls, ageing women with smooth young men, handsome couples plumbing the depths of each other's eyes, nibbling ears.

When I got home it was midnight. There

was Diana's beret in the hall and her music case which I picked up and went slowly up the stairs.

Tim was reading in bed with just the bedside lamp on so I hoped he wouldn't notice my sunburned face. He hadn't taken the bed-cover off, I usually did it, but must just have rolled it back and now it was in a heap on the floor. He said you're awfully late, darling, I was getting worried. I said sorry, I decided to stay in town to see that film with Audrey Hepburn, the weepy one you didn't want to see. He said alone and I said yes, my face in the bed-cover which I was folding. He said you hate going anywhere alone, why didn't you ring Martha and Jack? I said well I was just by the cinema so I thought I might as well.

He was excited about his merger and he told me about it while I undressed. How it was going to be quite something if it came off and what Maxwell Murray had said over the lobster. I took quite a long time taking my face off and going over the wonderful day with Dobbie. I wasn't really paying any attention to what he was saying until I realised it was quiet and he had put down his book and stopped talking. I said, frightened suddenly, Tim what's the matter? He said nothing, hurry up and come to bed.

We didn't go to Brighton again. The weather started to break up after that first time. I took to meeting Dobbie in town for lunch a couple of times a week. On the Wednesday after Brighton we went to Leoni's in Soho. Sitting at the next table was Archie Tindall. I wasn't surprised because I knew that sooner or later it was bound to happen. I was under the impression that Archie leered at me but since that was his permanent expression I wasn't sure. He knew Dobbie of course. We all had a little chat then Archie went back to his table and the man with whom he was lunching.

I knew I should have to tell Tim, Archie wasn't one for keeping anything to himself. I ran into Dobbie today in town, I said, he took me out to lunch. Don't tell me he does his shopping at Liberty's, Tim said. No, I was crossing Davies Street and he came by in the car. Haven't seen much of him lately, Tim said, why don't you ask him for dinner? He's going away next week, I said, when he comes back. Olga of course tried to make something of it.

'Darling, what on earth's going on?' she said when I met her in the fishmonger's. 'Do tell!'

I looked suitably innocent.

'You and Dobbie. Archie said you were terribly tête-à-tête.'

I laughed. 'You know Dobbie. He's always around.'

'I've always thought him an absolute dish,'

Olga said. 'I wish he'd come and hang around our house. Does he take you out much?'

'Don't be silly.' I examined my shopping list. 'Do you think they've any lemon soles?'

'Still waters,' Olga said. 'I won't breathe a word to Tim.'

'About the lunch?' I said. 'Tim knows.'

Olga looked disappointed.

'Anyway don't be ridiculous.'

'You've looked different lately,' Olga said. 'Radiant.'

'There's some over there.'

'What?'

'Lemon soles.'

'You don't have to worry about me. I'm the soul of discretion.' Soul and soles.

'For heaven's sake, Olga!' Not everyone's like you, I wanted to say. I went to ask the fishmonger in his white apron and rubber boots about the lemon soles and thought that perhaps they were, only to a lesser or greater degree.

She was looking at me speculatively over the slab and I could see that out of everybody Olga guessed.

Dobbie telephoned every morning. We talked about nothing in particular for a long time. He went to Italy and then to Spain. Robin caught the bug that was going round and had a week in bed. Suddenly it was November.

I'd seen him last on Wednesday. We'd had lunch and walked round a freezing park.

'This is ridiculous,' Dobbie said.

'I'll come up to the flat next week.' I hadn't been there since Brighton.

He stopped walking and looked at me.

'You mean it?'

I nodded. 'I thought perhaps it would wear itself out. It's got worse.'

He held me terribly close and I thought ridiculous, two middle-aged people in over-coats. I couldn't laugh off or ridicule the desperate need I had of Dobbie.

He dropped me off where I'd parked my car and said: 'Wednesday afternoon at the flat then, Liz. I can't manage lunch. I'll pick you up here at two.'

'Here' was a bomb-site car park where there was always room mid-week. I hated meeting Dobbie in restaurants. We'd found this place which had become our rendez-vous and as I drove up I was always relieved to find the broad nose of the Mercedes waiting outside.

'You'll ring me tomorrow?'

'I'm going to Czechoslovakia. First thing on Tuesday.'

The week had crawled by. Yesterday he'd rung and said all right for tomorrow Liz?

'More than all right,' I said. I couldn't think beyond it.

I waited all day for something to happen

as you always did with a home and children and you'd planned anything. Nothing went wrong. Mrs Mac seemed fit and Ted was in work and behaving and the children came home without any aches or pains.

I looked at Tim sitting in the armchair with the evening newspaper and said in my head I've been deceiving you for weeks and tomorrow afternoon I'm going to be unfaithful to you. He saw me looking at him and looked up at me and smiled. I smiled back, brazen enough even for that.

Now that the day had actually arrived I felt neither like a social outcast not terribly wicked. I had lived with the thought for so long that the deed was all but technically committed. I wasn't sure whether I regarded the adultery as a beginning or as an end. All I was certain of was that it was something I was in desperate need of to give my life, which lately had become meaningless, meaning. Where it would stop and if, what was to be the future tenor of my relationship with Dobbie, I refused to consider. I wanted to make love with him, wildly, savagely.

Twelve

I didn't really think I was going to be able to concentrate on a dress for Pamela Talbot's wedding on this day of days but there was time to try at least one shop before I had to meet Martha.

The clothes business was a game; sometimes I hated it intensely. Living in the village and being the wife of an accountant imposed certain social obligations. Life was punctuated by a series of evenings which presupposed clothes for the job; if you were the guest that was. If you were the hostess it presupposed a great deal more. It started generally with 'Isn't it time we had some people?' demanded casually of Tim; sometimes it emanated from Tim himself, 'Liz, we ought to ask the so-and-so's.' It wasn't difficult, viewed, casually dressed, from one's armchair, a dream hostess gracious and perfect from whom the guests would drift singing one's praises. In reality it was an uphill grind starting with the invitations on the telephone, the unimportant ones leaping at it and the vital planets in the galaxy uncertain. You weren't sure then whether to call the whole thing off, for another day, or carry on until you were too committed and all you could do was hope. The component parts in order, more or less, the next step was to set about turning one's home into a palace, oneself into a queen. There were lists; scraps of paper, losing themselves all over the house, having to do with cocktail cherries and so many bridge rolls and extra pastry forks from Martha. The lists became translated with time into laden cardboard boxes in the kitchen; from the greengrocer's with tomatoes and radishes and cucumber; from the grocer's with anchovies and pickled onions and coffee sugar; and into silver from the cupboard where it was put away in polythene and into paper serviettes and into doilies. The silver, the linen, the glass; flowers to be arranged, would they open too soon in the central heating? Little dishes with peppermint creams, jellies, nuts; cigarettes and ashtrays; olives, cheese straws, potato crisps. The lampshades should have been washed, I'd been meaning to; a broken cup, one of the best; rain and mud on the hall carpet on the day. Was it worth it? What are you going to so much trouble for, Tim said, just because Olga does? If you're doing it you have to do it properly. Everything ready. Mrs Mac with a long face because of the extra work casting a shadow; Tim and the children helping themselves to sweets, to nuts, disturbing the cushions. The desire to run.

Suddenly it was over. The sack of Carthage, the splendour that was Rome. Grey-filled ashtrays and choking air, cress on the grey carpet and cream from the cake; pools of wet on the sideboard and crumpled paper napkins; disordered pastries, a half-eaten bridge roll, olive stones in the hearth. In the hall mirror, dismembering the final remnants of a smile, giving way to the fatigue that had been clamouring for the past hour with surreptitious glances at the clock, wondering when they were going. There was a moment of triumph, when it was all worth it. Somewhere about eleven o'clock with everyone eating and drinking and smoking and laughing and saying how marvellous Liz, did you honestly make it? You look younger than ever, Tim too, and give such marvellous parties. Animated, you believed it. Then they were gone and with them the hope that something had been achieved. With the closing of the door the isolation returned. The hollowness of nothing gained except for the burn on the bookcase, the broken glass, and the repair work which would go on for the rest of the week. The crushing burden of tomorrow.

The dress helped. If it was right you grew wings, could reach fantastic heights. If it was a failure then so were you, doomed from the outset, brooding all evening, humiliated. You told yourself it was unimportant, it was personality that counted. You lied in your teeth. It was important; desperately. So you played the game, accepted the bondage of elegance. Like the upkeep of the home it was a constant battle against deterioration. We had to struggle with so many side issues and live as well; men got away scot free.

In the lives of some of the girls in the village it was more than a side issue. They thought of nothing else. Olga, I knew, before she even started on the clothes, spent hours raising herself on tiptoe without touching the floor with her heels in order to slender- ise her ankles, put oil on her fingernails, crushed strawberries on her cheeks. She didn't drink because it was bad for her skin, avoided the sun on her face for a similar reason, brushed her hair a hundred times, became hysterical if she missed her afternoon rest. I didn't go to quite such lengths in order to preserve my attraction. Attraction for whom? It couldn't have been for Tim because Tim loved me anyway, in anything; more often than not he was blind to what I was wearing. Who did we dress for? It wasn't for Dobbie because I'd always taken trouble and there'd only recently been Dobbie. Other women? In a way I suppose; vying, demonstrating our sophistication, youth; more likely for their husbands, making them jealous; look at Liz, lucky Tim; boosting our self-esteem. We stayed younger longer. Our mothers, grandmothers at any rate, at our age had given up. The longer you battled the harder it grew, the more time it was necessary to devote. Figure preservation was the latest thing. Half the girls in the village spent two afternoons, sometimes three, in town, in black leotards, battering their buttocks with rollers, strapped and swinging against various pieces of equipment, beating themselves endlessly against others. They swore it worked. Martha went and said you could get the same result much cheaper doing the various exercises at home. I put my fingertips together and pressed to improve my bust whenever I remembered. Fortunately I was slim and clothes weren't too much of a problem.

I parked the car, lucky to find a meter, a chauffeur with a black Bentley pulled out just near to where I wanted to go, and prepared for battle with the dress shop. The battle consisted in being prepared not to be talked into something you didn't want. The assistants worked on commission; their job was to sell dresses. It didn't matter to them if in the dress they declared ravishing you felt a dismal flop. The success of their stratagems depended on your mood. Today it would take more than a saleswoman to intimidate me. I was going to meet my lover.

I took off my driving shoes, ancient moccasins, and put on my heels, and sixpence, listening to the satisfying whirr, in the meter.

In the window there was a turquoise chiffon dress, quite gorgeous with coat to match, unpriced. On the floor lay a jersey two-piece, not unsmart, the come-on marked at seven guineas.

Iris Sayers had told me about the shop which she said didn't have to be wildly expensive although they had some exclusive models, and where she was usually successful. I was to ask for Miss Forrest.

I opened the door and was aware of being priced up by four pairs of eyes. The owner of one of them came forward smiling calculatingly. I explained what I was looking for and whom. The interest evaporated, it was not her day. She turned to a thin superior type in a Chanel suit. 'Miss Forrest, Modom's looking for a smart little cocktail.'

Miss Forrest came forward looking down her long nose. 'About what praice?'

'I don't really know. I'd like to see what you have.'

I lost a point for not answering the question. With disdain she pulled aside a curtain.

'Has Modom any preference for colour?'

'No. I've an open mind.'

She took out a pale blue crepe, draped at the hip.

'Not blue.'

She took it back and exchanged it for

183

black, similarly draped.

'I don't care for draping.'

She held it against her and you could see she wouldn't be seen dead in it. 'Of course they look quaite different in the hand.'

'But drapes. I'm not the drapey type.'

The next one was scarlet, smart but shrieking. Miss Forrest looked at my face.

'They're all wearing it.'

'It drains my colour.'

'With a little more make-up…'

I'd look like a clown.

White with beads.

'I don't care for beading. Something plainer, with a line rather than decoration.'

She returned the white to its plastic cover with much ado and produced a black with a high neck and low back, elegant and simple.

'That's more like it.'

'Now we're getting a little more praicey,' she said doubtfully.

I looked at the ticket; she hadn't been deceived by the mink tie.

Out of nowhere, sensing difficulty, the manageress came, chic, from the Continent.

'Modom's looking for a smart little cocktail. She doesn't care for drapes or beading or blues or reds,' was the indictment.

With an air of authority the manageress produced a brown velvet and swept the moss-green carpet with it.

'Somesing quite fabulous,' she said, gesticulating, 'wiz a brooch 'ere and brown shoes, *voilà!*'

'I don't think it's within Modom's praice range,' Miss Forrest said, changing allegiance. 'I've shown most of the ones that were and she doesn't care for them.'

I refused to hang my head.

'I show you somesing,' the manageress said in a conspiratorial voice. She delved behind another curtain and came out with a green wool suit.

'Frrrench and on-re-peat-able. A tiny size. Take Madame to ze fitting-room. You will see, Madame.'

'It's lovely,' I said, and it was, the price was right too, but I wanted a dress for Pamela Talbot's wedding.

'I can hardly wear it for a wedding.'

'Terribly chic. Ze colour, ze braid, and wiz Madame's eyes...'

'But I wanted a cocktail dress.'

She whispered in my ear. 'In Paris zey wear ze suit for everyzing. A brooch 'ere...'

Green shoes ... it was a glorious suit. I was in the fitting-room, my clothes off, the suit zipped and fastened.

She threw up her hands. 'What can I say? Walk outside, Madame.'

The three witches led by Miss Forrest purred fabulous.

I forced myself back to the fitting-room and removed the suit.

'I'm sorry. It's very nice but I want a cocktail dress.'

'Wiz a velvet blouse, ze same green, black shoes ... *formidable*...' The manageress walked away leaving me with Miss Forrest who watched in silence as I dressed.

In silence like a naughty schoolgirl she led me out of the fitting-room and across the floor. On her way she shut the curtain on the blue with drapes, the white beaded.

'Perhaps you'll be having some more in,' I said, warm now having undressed and dressed and feeling dishevelled.

'I don't think you'll find a better selection...' Her voice was chilly. She held open the door, waiting.

I pointed to the chiffon in the window.

'What's the price of that, it's gorgeous?'

'French.'

Of course.

'Unrepeatable.'

Naturally.

'Seventy-faive guineas. Without the coat, of course.'

So much for Iris Sayers and her recommendations. I never had been able to buy anything with those dreadful women breathing down my neck and preferred to shop where I was known or at a store near Marble Arch where they had cheap copies of Paris models and you could riffle through and try on to your heart's content, nobody caring.

186

It was an effort to keep in the swim and it didn't end with the dress. You had shoes to get, a struggle for fit and colour, a handbag more often than not and sometimes a special foundation. Like small girls playing at dressing up we decked ourselves out like fairy queens and identified ourselves with our finery. Most of us at any rate. There was one sect in the village led by Myrtle Appleton whose husband was our local dentist who wallowed in suburban intellectualism and sat on the floor until all hours exchanging second-hand opinions on Mahler and Brecht. They pretended to like nothing that was straightforward and freeflowing, only the obscure, no matter how fifth-rate, and going to off-beat little cinemas or theatres and barefoot, as if this made them morally superior. They joined a two-guinea Society where all the pseudo-intellectuals had the pleasure of meeting other pseudo-intellectuals. I call them pseudos. Had they been the real thing they wouldn't have had to convince themselves with their pseudo-exclusive Society but would have been too busy using these wonderful brains instead of sitting around gassing. Myrtle herself, hair long or flung up on her head, strands trailing, dressed in odd clothes made out of saris or antique fabrics and decorated herself with ancient beads evoking the Middle Ages or old China. She despised us, we knew, for our slavish devotion to the ordinances of fashion yet probably spent more time rummaging for her old bits of jade and amber than we did chasing the more conventional. As the years went by the more impossible to talk to Myrtle became. Everything had to be 'anti'; music, poetry, and heroes. Tim said it was to compensate for marrying a dentist.

In the car I put on my driving shoes again, throwing the others on to the back seat, and drove off to meet Martha. If I found a meter straight away I should be just in time. The lunch hour was always difficult.

The fog was clearing but there were wisps of it still in places. The traffic, streets, everything looked grey. I drove down Berkeley Street, Davies Street, and Wigmore Street. There was a Hillman Minx in front of me going very slowly, obviously looking for a meter too. Two women in hats sat in the front nattering and I kept well back as Tim had taught me, knowing that they were quite likely at any moment to catch sight of something in a shop window and pull up sharply or veer to the left as a preliminary to a right turn. There was no space at all in Wigmore Street, every meter bay neatly occupied with its car. I decided to turn left. The Hillman did too and beat me to one in Wimpole Street.

I drove on exasperated. Manchester

Square then Portman Square, getting further and further away. I could see it was one of those days and going to be hopeless and thought I might as well go straight to the car park where I was meeting Dobbie and leave the car there. I parked it safely and coming out over the rough gravel which I felt through my thin-soled shoes I looked at the spot outside where in less than two hours Dobbie's car would be and thought that by the time I drove my own car away I wouldn't be the same person at all.

There was a taxi passing and I hailed it sliding with relief on to the leather seat.

Martha was sitting crossly in Bendick's in the mink coat Jack had given her after his last successful coup and said where on earth did you get to I've read the menu forty-four and a half times.

'There was nowhere to park.'

'I always leave mine in Selfridge's. It saves a lot of bother. Where did you?'

'A bomb-site, miles from here.'

'I'll drop you off on the way to Dr Raus.'

'I have something to do first.'

'My appointment's not until three, I'll come with you.'

'It's nothing terribly interesting.'

'All right, darling. I can take a hint. You're very mysterious I must say.'

It was a mistake to have arranged to meet Martha.

'Am I?' I picked up the menu. 'What are we going to eat?'

Martha put on her glasses which had gold sides. 'I had half a grapefruit and black coffee with Saxin this morning and we've steak with apple chiffon, which I adore, tonight; that comes to three hundred and fifty allowing for two helpings of the chiffon which I know I shall have to have, leaving me with nine hundred to play around with.'

I waited patiently not really caring today about her hips. She rejected with reluctance the *oeufs florentine* and the scrambled egg with asparagus tips and settled for the cheese and date salad which, with a bit of cheating, she didn't count the roll and butter she had to have because she was starving, left her with enough calories in hand for the chocolate fudge sundae, the *specialité de la maison*.

'What about you?'

It really didn't matter, I was too worked up over Dobbie. Now that the moment was at hand I felt apprehensive and excited, eager and reluctant, all at once.

'I'll just have a sandwich.'

'Are you all right?'

'Perfectly. Just not terribly hungry.'

The waitress waited with her little book.

'That's one cheese and date with roll and butter and one sandwich,' Martha said.

'No sandwiches between twelve and two.'

I opened the menu again. 'Buck rarebit.

And coffee.'

'You remember Jessica Chatterton,' Martha said.

By her tone of voice I knew somebody had died or had cancer.

'Wasn't that the commercial art girl Gray used to take out?'

'That was Margot, her sister. Jessica was the one with red hair. The very tall one. You must remember. Used to go skating every Sunday.'

'What about her?'

'It's not her, it's her husband. She married that queer-looking fellow from the Polytechnic. He didn't have a bean and there was all that carry-on at the time.'

I remembered now about Jessica.

'He never did have a bean either,' Martha said, 'everything he touched went wrong. Anyway, they'd been visiting her people. Her father's that old bore on the local council. They'd just got home and were getting undressed when Tom said I feel frightfully odd and dropped down dead at her feet.'

I tried to feel for Jessica Chatterton only of course she wasn't Jessica Chatterton any more.

'They've three children under five,' Martha said, 'or perhaps it's four. I know they seem to have another one every time you pick up the *Telegraph*. I don't know what she'll do poor soul.'

'Shocking,' I said. And playing the game. 'Who told you?'

'Iris. She was the only one she kept in touch with. Iris' mother hasn't been too well either. She had this pain and they took out something and she still had the pain, so they opened her up again and had a look round and couldn't find an absolute thing. They've called in somebody else but meanwhile she still had the pain. Iris is terribly worried.'

The waitress brought our order, the butter in its individual earthenware pot.

'There's always something,' Martha said. 'You never know from one day to the next. I've got to take Robert to the specialist, he complains of pains in his feet.'

'Is his eye better?'

'Yes, they said to take no notice and that it would correct itself. I hope to goodness they're right. Jack has a cold coming on, he gets one every November.'

'He was all right last night.'

'He had a tickle all evening. This morning he was sneezing his head off. He'll be furious if he's not fit for Saturday, there's some sort of competition. Is Tim playing?'

'I haven't heard about it. It's possible.'

'Unless of course it's foggy.' Martha looked out of the window and people were passing by with umbrellas and it was pouring with rain and I'd neither a scarf nor umbrella. I didn't want to meet Dobbie looking a mess.

'I thought it would,' Martha said. 'Anyway it will clear the last of the fog.'

Martha enjoyed her chocolate sundae which had all the appeal of forbidden fruit. I had coffee with a Danish pastry and looked constantly at my watch, watching the minutes creep nearer and nearer to two and hoping I would be able to get a taxi back to the car park.

Martha was on about the straw-coloured walls and curtains again so I could just say yes or no every so often and think about Dobbie and that if Martha knew what was in my mind she'd have a fit and enough to gossip about till doomsday.

We asked for the bill and time was getting on now so I'd have to hurry. I went downstairs to tidy up my face while Martha waited for it. When I came back the waitress still hadn't brought it and I began to get agitated because of the rain and it mightn't be so easy to get a taxi and Dobbie would be waiting so I said do you mind awfully Martha if I go? She said where's the fire and I said it's nearly two and I need to get somewhere before it closes. It sounded ridiculous as I said it because everything closed for lunch at one if it was going to and opened again at two. Martha said all right, I'm not in a rush, and why don't you come in tonight? Not doing anything are you? Tonight seemed such a long way off. Two o'clock was the edge of the world and I couldn't think any further so I said, I'm not certain, I'll ring you, and stepped into Wigmore Street and into the rain forgetting to pay for my lunch.

PART TWO

One

Rain, with a sharp tug at memory, always took me back to the day Tim and I became engaged. It was hard to believe that between then and now nineteen years, somewhere, somehow, had passed. 'A thousand ages in Thy sight are like an evening gone.' *Time and the Conways*. It was a curious thing, time; you never knew what had happened to it except when you were young and it dragged. The party or holiday you were waiting for seemed never to come nearer. In winter the summer was a lifetime away; when it did arrive it promised falsely to endure for ever. Now time had wings; seven-league boots, too. When Tim and I got married people celebrating Silver Weddings were out of our orbit. Now we were well on the way ourselves. Years number one to fifteen of marriage were the delusory ones, the ones in which you painlessly changed from identification with the bride to that of the bride's mother when you went to a wedding. You could not pinpoint the precise spot. At one moment you were dreaming up

195

the aisle, moved to tears by Lohengrin, sure that all was going to be hearts and flowers, and the next you were imagining it was your own daughter leaving the nest, the desire to be taken with tugging at you. Somewhere along the line the emphasis subtly shifted. You were a child, then you were your own mother. You recognised her gestures in your mirror; understood with clarity, what it was all about.

Things like photographs put the dipstick into the sands of time. Ours were kept theoretically in an album, but actually in a collection of cardboard boxes and carrier bags. They were filled to overflowing with a miscellany of prints, coloured and black-and-white, straight and deckle-edged, from home and abroad. They ranged from Robin and Diana naked on rugs as babies, we never remembered to write names and dates so often couldn't be sure which was which, through their first garden swing, Robin in rompers, to Diana, complete with hat, on our recent Italian jaunt. Tim had changed from a slight, almost emaciated young man to a more stolid edition with slightly receding hair. I had progressed through ludicrously long and dowdy hair and skirts to the fashion of the day, which tomorrow would be equally ridiculous.

There was one photograph of Tim and me in the early days on the beach at Bognor, leaping up to catch a ball. It perpetuated a moment you knew was irretrievably gone. Moments, too, were preserved in our boxes of those whose days were numbered. Tim's Aunt Millicent enjoying tomato sandwiches in our garden. Had she known that two weeks later she was to fall and die as the result of a fractured femur she would not have grinned so broadly. David, gap-toothed, from Robin's class who had dashed across the road under a bus. My Uncle Rupert, importantly paunched, who had seemed so indispensable at the Bar, struck down by a cerebral haemorrhage. These faces put the thumbprints upon the passage of the years. Their images, captured in Kodacolor, now gone, brought home the evanescence of our days.

In the nineteen years that had come and passed we had been engaged and married, improved our financial position, reared two children, and moved house. Looking back it did not seem possible that we had actually lived, making decisions, from day to day through so many years. Like a dream they slipped irrevocably by. Sometimes, alerted to sudden awareness of their passing, by birthdays or christenings or anniversaries or deaths, I determined to treat the days less lightly, seize them with either hand. It was no good. There was too much to think about. Too much to do. They became consumed in a busy-ness of living, fragmented by the constant effort to keep up with commitments; education and clothes and dentists and haircuts and holidays and homework and insurance and income and income-tax and entertainment and illness and charity and the elements and curtains and carpets and new accounts for Tim and maids and dailies and saving for the children's future and pipes that burst and central heating and trees to be lopped and the scare of smallpox and bus strikes and the general trauma of everyday life. It seemed a physical impossibility to keep track of the days let alone to nurture them.

We had had thoughts now and again, like everyone, of getting off the treadmill; of emigrating to California where at least you hadn't the worry of keeping warm or to the peace of the countryside. It was nothing but a pipedream though, recurring every so often. We knew that no matter where we went the problems would come with us and that we were not alone on the hurdy-gurdy; it was the price of civilisation.

The business of time had always intrigued me. My grandmother who died just after the war having remained, as the old often did, quite unmoved by it except as it touched her own comfort, had I knew to clean her knives with paste, no stainless steel then, to wash up without benefit of detergents, let alone mechanical aid, to physically haul her washing and water in and out of the copper, which I remember stood in her basement, and to grind her own salt. She gave birth, the hard way, no gas-and-air machine, to seven children, reared five of them and was as far as I remembered a woman of great serenity. We had photographs of her sitting sedately in her garden beneath a tree, on a hard chair, looking as if she had not a care in the world. I did half as much with twice as much assistance and still there seemed scarcely a moment to breathe. Even my mother ran a contemplative finger over the synthetic surfaces of my equipment, searched for rubbish to put, fascinated, down the waste-grinder, and mused on the number of dishes and napkins she had washed or had caused to be washed over the years. What I wanted to know was the whereabouts of the great chunks of leisure I should have had at my disposal. True I could get out of the house for short spells but usually rushing somewhere for something, neither appreciating nor putting to good use the gifts of time donated by Mrs Mac, and the automation with which I was surrounded. Tim was not the sort of husband who demanded to know what I had done with every minute of my day; sometimes I would have found it hard to tell him. The dishes were washed automatically and so were the clothes, dried too, the rooms dusted and Hoovered by Mrs Mac. The things I actually did seemed so trivial yet took so long. Often I tried to think what they were, these nebulous, ever-present chores that rose from the vacuum created by the machinery to occupy me and others like me in the village. They could be said in a breath, quickly. Each task however took its five, ten, or fifteen minutes from the day. The time-motion studies which were always being done on behalf of the housewife took into account the obvious jobs such as bedmaking, cooking and cleaning. They did not allow for putting out dead flowers, picking up the trail of petals you dropped on the way, counting the laundry, trying frustratedly to get it all into the box, making lists, of groceries to be bought, jobs to do, telephoning dentists for appointments, service departments of machinery that had gone wrong, taking things upstairs that had found their way downstairs and vice-versa, suits to be pressed, taken, and collected, shoes to be mended, two journeys likewise, hair to be cut, clothes to be purchased, altered, repaired, plants to be watered, leaves cleansed with milk, parcels sorted for jumble, for Oxfam, broken shoelaces, burned saucepans, upset buttons or pins, prescriptions at the chemists, birthday presents for Robin's friends, Diana's, their own parties to be organised; most of all they turned an oblivious eye on the eternal tidying; pieces of string and brown paper and torn-out recipes and paper bags of things to go back to the stores and hair bands and guns and gloves and macs and boots and books and swimming costumes and dried-up Grip-fix. Every day was filled; seven of them to a week. It seemed to be always Monday or Friday and suddenly Easter approaching and last summer's clothes not fitting, then summer and winter again, jumpers washed beyond redemption, wrists out of heavy coats, and Christmas to worry about, presents and Brussels sprouts, and almost before your fork was out of the Christmas pudding, spring. There should have been a button to slow it all down. At the rate we were going I felt that in no time I would be looking at a wrinkled face in the mirror and thinking with panic, this cannot be me. That was if I grew to be wrinkled. So many of our acquaintances seemed to be having breasts removed or coronary thromboses, one, two, three and then it was poor old John or Jennie, never had a day's illness in their lives, conversation meat for a while then nothing. We might all, of course, be nothing quite shortly, in spite of all the marching, in which case the whole thing, everything, was a complete waste anyway so it really didn't matter how you filled your days.

If the time in years since my engagement to Tim had gone like a tape wound at speed the difference between the two worlds, then and now, was so great it would not have been surprising if the years that separated them had been twice that number. The war, although we did not know it, was drawing to its close. We lived in a world of ration books and points and blackouts and careless talk costing lives. At night we could see a vague glow in the sky from the incendiaries they dropped on London. We didn't know about nylon stockings, drip-dry or instant anything, bananas, cream, biscuits in lovely shiny packets, bicycles for birthdays, holidays abroad, or many of the other things we took for granted today. After nineteen years the dried milk, powdered eggs, and liquid paraffin with which we cooked were only a joke as were the Spitfires, Mosquitoes, and Hurricanes, with which we fought and prevailed. To Robin and Diana the era was as remote as the Middle Ages. When Tim and I laughed about it, remembering the funny side, the other was too grim, families left with telegrams when it was over instead of sons, it assumed a fairy-tale-like quality too.

In the village to which I had been evacuated I went to school. Most of the girls in the sixth form and many of the younger ones too – it was a status symbol to wear somebody's wings or anchor – had boyfriends in the services. Our talk was peppered with expression such as give me the gen, bags of panic, what a wizzo place, good show, piece of cake, cutting a rug, had it; terms which had died a lingering death in post-war England breathing their last when people like Tim, even today, after so many years got excited. We danced, with each other in the gym, to sentimental tunes like *Spring will be a little late this year*, jived to *Holiday for Strings*, collected salvage indefatigably, saw films like *The Way Ahead*, *Henry V* and *Since You Went Away*. We could laugh now with the chasm almost as great as that from the nineteen-fourteen lot. The rubble had been razed and from the dung-heap our cold-war, nuclear-threatening, twisting, with-it, Continent-hopping, teddy-boy-infested generation had arisen; Robin and Diana's world; what would they do with it?

The highlights of my life at that time were letters from Tim, whose wings I wore proudly on my blazer, and his leaves. The letters bore the legend on active service, the stamp of the censor, and Tim's rank and number. I still had them. They were strangely lacking in terms of actual news. You could feel the censor breathing over his shoulder. From them I learned that the life somewhere in Europe was one of great, stifling tedium, except when there was a job on, meaning a raid somewhere, and that Tim had become a war-weary zombie, interested only in baths and sleep and getting out and that he loved me, missed me, and clung for reason and sanity to my image. I kept his in a silver frame, by my bed.

Looking back, the demarcation between peace and war existed only palely. It seemed that at one moment we were leading our untroubled existence in Wimbledon, Tim, Gray, and I and occasionally Dobbie, having graduated from Monopoly to rummy and billiards on Saturday afternoons, and the next everything had been shaken up. Gray went off to the Army leaving our mother in a perpetual state of alarm and despondency, Tim to the Air Force, eventually to find himself with Dobbie his Commanding Officer, and myself to a strange country school. When Gray went away my mother cried at the coarse uniform and the heavy boots and every time they played *Ma, I miss your apple pie* on the radio. She hated to think of him roughing it although Gray didn't mind a bit. We stopped needling each other, Gray and I, and grew up suddenly and began talking to each other as adults. When he came on leave he usually brought with him two or three other spotty young servicemen with ridiculous army haircuts. They were grateful for all my mother was able to provide them with out of the rations and seemed not to know what to do with their clumsy feet. It was odd to see Gray shining his own boots, there had always been someone to do it for him and with his hands red and roughened from the various fatigues he had to do. He changed gradually, from leave to leave, from a soft-looking schoolboy to a soldier with the muscles of a navvy. He came home fairly regularly at first then he said I may not be seeing you for a bit, Ma. He disappeared for two years during which time Mother's hair turned white. There weren't any tints and rinses then, of course, so she stayed that way, looking years younger now than she did then, worrying about Gray and crying into the butter ration when she thought no-one was looking.

Before they all joined up Tim and I were together a lot but usually with a group when he wasn't at our house. There was Gray and a Frank Hankin who was going to be a play-wright and was killed at Dunkirk. There was Irene Douglas, who lived round the corner, and was my best friend and married a clean young American from West Point. She now lived in Los Angeles from where we corres-ponded spasmodically. The clean young American had become an executive in a large family candy concern. Whenever I thought of Irene it was sitting on the edge of a pool, her own, with two clean American children, in the yard of her clean American home, without a care in the sun-drenched world.

At that time we all belonged to a youth

club. We had play readings and earnest discussions and I danced cheek to cheek with Tim who took me home. In the summer we went on rambles into the country. We took the train to the nearest point, meeting early at the station with our rucksacks, and walked. After lunch we paired off and it was usually me and Tim, Gray with a variety of girls. We'd lie on the grass and talk about ourselves and what we were going to do and tickle each other with blades of grass and kiss with adolescent innocence. Afterwards suffused with warmth and delight, we'd walk back with arms round each other's waists.

When Tim joined up I went to the station. Now I couldn't go to Waterloo or Paddington or any of the other main lines without thinking of that day. The platforms were jam-packed with a milling, moving mass of grey and khaki loaded with lumpy packs. Wherever you looked people were surging towards trains and buffets, or clinging to each other. Girls with square-shouldered dresses and shoulder length hair entwined themselves around their men with tears rolling down despairing faces. Mothers cried unashamedly, fathers looked embarrassed. For the most part the men themselves appeared bewildered. Tim's mother hadn't come, she didn't like stations, his father was in Ireland on Government business; only Gray and I. His uniform was very new. He'd gone through the preliminary stages and now was going away for training somewhere in the North. When it was time to go he said goodbye to Gray and turned to me. I felt a bit awkward because of Gray then Tim put his arms round me and I didn't any more and we were clinging to each other like everyone else and kissing ferociously. I promised to write and Tim said he'd miss me. Our kisses were different, desperate and afraid, though innocent still. He was my man going to war, my thing to live for. I was his girl.

After that there were letters and leaves and hours spent on the stairs in each other's arms and walking, as one, in the blackout. At school I found it difficult to concentrate sometimes, knowing he was waiting. Our letters and our meetings became more and more intense until both of us could think of little else.

The school, which was in the village, was two miles away from the little house we had rented. I often thought when Robin and Diana went off in the car how horrified they'd be if they had to walk two miles any-where, let alone twice a day to school. We'd been rehearsing a play, *Two Gentlemen of Verona,* in which I was Julia. It was pitch dark when I got out, because of no street lights and the blackout, and pouring, but really pouring with rain. I had my torch with the blue paper covering the bulb as stipulated but could scarcely see an inch ahead. The village was deserted, everyone indoors at their tea. After I'd walked about a mile up the hill towards home I was fed up and completely soaked, my feet squelching in every puddle on the muddy road. My torch was almost useless and my satchel weighed a ton. Perhaps when I got home there would be a letter from Tim.

I turned a corner and a figure loomed up in front of me. I said sorry and side-stepped. You were always bumping into people in the blackout. A familiar voice said, Liz, and it was Tim.

I was never so glad to see anyone. I dropped my satchel in a puddle and we stood there in each other's arms the rain pelting down. We rubbed our wet faces together kissing and I had never been so happy. It was some time before I noticed there was something different about him then I saw it was the peaked cap and knew that he'd been made an officer.

'I wasn't expecting you.'
'Embarkation leave.'
'No.'
'Yes.'
'Liz. I love you.'
'I love you.' I was bursting with love, the rain and my wetness completely forgotten. I could just make out his face in the darkness.

'We'll get married won't we, Liz?'

'Of course.'

'As soon as it's all over.'

We kissed.

'Joey bought it yesterday. Over Cologne.'

'Joey Dench?' Baby-face Joey.

'Yes. It helps to have you.'

'Are you afraid?'

'Petrified. Every time I go up. We all hate it.'

'It will soon be over.'

'Not soon enough.'

He picked up my satchel and put his arm round me and we walked slowly, happily through the puddles, not minding the rain. I was seventeen.

Two

The rain fell on to the pavements of Wigmore Street and bounced off them again. I stood under the lee of the shops and made advances to every taxi I saw. Every single one had somebody in as always seemed to be the case when it was raining. I could feel my hairdo, which had looked so nice, disintegrating in the damp and decided that even though it was ten to two I had better go into Debenham's and buy an umbrella. Had I not being going to meet Dobbie I would have gone to the haberdashery for one of those plastic rain-hats but I couldn't turn up looking like a boiled sweet for our assignation. I had come a long way since the night I became engaged to Tim. I hadn't thought twice then about the fact that my hair was plastered to my face like a wet spaniel's, my nose rinsed clean as a beacon. This was Wigmore Street, not a country lane, and I belonged to the affluent society. I had two perfectly good umbrellas at home and didn't want anything too expensive. The assistant tried to sell me a very elegant one with a tortoiseshell handle that went with Madam's coat and cost seven guineas; failing that one of the telescopic variety which I never seemed to be able to untelescope at the crucial moment. She seemed quite upset when I decided on a plain red. It wasn't really the colour I wanted but was the cheapest they had and would probably end up going to school with Diana. It was five to and I hadn't the correct money. She seemed to write the bill out deliberately slowly then disappeared on varicose-veined legs through handkerchiefs and stockings in search of change. It seemed she had gone for lunch while she was at it but she did eventually return. We thanked each other profusely, smiled, hope it would stop raining soon, and agreed that it was better than the fog, anything was better than the fog. It was a minute to two. Outside it was really overcast now, the rain looking as if it was in for the afternoon. A taxi pulled up outside John Bell & Croyden letting someone out. I raised the red umbrella and shouted and attempted to cross but the lights were against me. I thought the driver had seen me and was waiting and was relieved I wasn't going to be very late for Dobbie. When I reached the other side of the road I was in time to see a man dash from the shelter of the shops and into the taxi. My shoes, which were black snake-skin, were soaked. I knew there must be mud splashed up the backs of my legs. I felt thoroughly cold and damp and just a little hysterical and imagined Dobbie drawing up at the car park, it was just on two, and looking at his watch. There seemed nothing for it but to walk as quickly as I could. It would take a good ten minutes, I could have done it in less in flat shoes. Perhaps I would be able to pick up a taxi on the way.

I set off quickly, the rain dripping off the red umbrella, thinking of Dobbie waiting and if he would think I wasn't going to turn up, had cold feet or something. That was funny, cold feet, he would soon find out. It would have been better if it hadn't been cold. In summer it would probably have seemed less calculated, the sun hot, warming everything, less clothes, the exhilarated feeling that the crisp air gave you instead of this chilling drip drip. I tried to protect my handbag beneath the umbrella, progressing as fast as possible. The rain was driving directly towards me so that if I held the umbrella to protect my face I couldn't see where I was going. The taxis were passing at speed all of them occupied. Normally I would have stopped to look at the shops. I hardly saw them trying to keep the rain off and not to collide with anyone. The post office clock said three minutes past two. I wasn't doing at all badly, must have been walking faster than I thought. I eased up a bit. I wasn't going to be more than ten minutes late and didn't want to arrive in too much of a state. Picturing Dobbie sitting in the car, smoking probably, perhaps listening to the radio while he waited. I had a sudden urge to run to him, to be there, right away, in his arms, secure, removed from Mrs Mac and Robin and Diana and Martha and even Tim; somewhere where no-one could find me until I chose to emerge. Dobbie, I said aloud. No-one could see beneath the umbrella. If they did they would just think me a little mad. People often walked along talking to themselves, you just smiled. Dobbie! I won't be long. I speeded up again and was about to cross Orchard Street when the lights changed to red. I stood impatiently on the edge of the kerb with the dripping crowd while the rain swilled down the gutter and the cars and taxis, indicator lights flashing redly right and left, passed wetly by. People behind waiting to cross pushed up almost into the flooded gutter. No-one wanted to stand around in the downpour. An old lady next to me in a navy gabardine mac with a plastic rain-hood decorated with daisies over her grey hair teetered on the edge of the kerb. The rain streamed from the edge of her hood, down her glasses and on to her nose. She was peering up at the lights and I suppose she thought they had changed to green because before I realised she was stepping into the road, head down. All at once, instead of just the steady hiss of the traffic and the people waiting to cross Portman Square, everything was in a turmoil. What happened first I'm not sure. There was a red Jaguar approaching fast from Baker Street to get across before the lights changed and this old lady stepping in its path and suddenly a tremendous screech of brakes and crumpling metal and screams and soaking water splayed to the knees. Then the old lady was lying quietly in her gabardine in the middle of the road. The red Jaguar was sideways on. The people from the kerb were horror-struck momentarily then were rushing past me. The old lady's handbag, brown plastic, lay in the rain-filled gutter at my feet.

I often dreamed about or imagined accidents particularly when we were going on holiday by air. For days before I had misgivings. The plane would crash and we would all end up scattered in little pieces against a mountainside or in the sea. I'd wonder how Tim and I could be so criminally negligent as to involve Robin and Diana, who had no choice, in the risk. There was more chance, Tim said, of having an accident in the car. Even crossing the road the risk was greater than going round the world I don't know how many times by air. I was unimpressed by the statistics which I knew to be impeccable. All I was aware of was that the week we planned to go away there always seemed to be some ghastly plane crash in the Persian Gulf or Arizona, usually in an identical plane to that we were to travel in. Tim said better still; it lowered the chances of our plane coming down. This particular piece of logic I never understood at all. Tim said I should have been flying during the war when things were coming at you from all sides and that going to Italy in a Comet or a Boeing was an absolute piece of cake. In the car crashes I dreamed of, going of course at speed, I was usually the victim. I could bear the image of myself lying spread-eagled in the road looking with serenity at the clouds with faceless people tutting softly, sympathetically above; or pinned beneath the steering wheel in my own car, wondering painlessly if I should ever walk again. Other people's accidents I walked quickly by. Years ago there had been a child under a bus. I remember the driver's face as he stood in the roadway, completely grey, and had gone home to be sick. I always prayed there would be others at hand to help. I had learned First Aid at Guides where we'd had great fun bandaging each other's healthy limbs. They hadn't taught us what to do with a smashed skull gushing blood or a grotesquely twisted limb.

From nowhere the ambulance had come and policemen. I was alone on the kerb. The rest of the crowd was in the middle of the road jostling for position in the rain.

The handbag was still in the gutter. I picked it up. There was no weight to it. It was probably precious to the old lady, might help to identify her if necessary. I pushed my way through the crowd holding the red umbrella aloft and trying not to tangle with the others of various colours which protected some of the onlookers from the rain. It was coming down harder than ever on to up-turned collars and dripping trilbies. A stretcher on which lay the old lady, covered with a horrible red blanket dark with rain spots, was disappearing into the back of the ambulance. Three police officers took down a statement from a woman in a beaver coat who kept saying 'she just stepped into the road, my God she must be crazy', and was on the verge of hysteria. I presumed she had been driving the Jag.

'Step back if you please, madam,' a constable with a dripping cape said, coming at me with arms wide. 'On the pavement if you please.'

'Her handbag.' I held it aloft and pointed towards the ambulance with my umbrella. 'This is her handbag. She dropped it when she was knocked down.'

He nodded briefly allowing me under his arm and turned his attention to the rest of the gawpers.

I peered into the ambulance, everyone

taking no notice of the constable except to shuffle back a few steps, and looking to see what I was up to. All the way up Baker Street traffic was hooting and everything seemed to be in a considerable state of confusion.

In the ambulance a man and a woman in navy blue uniforms were bending over the old lady.

'Excuse me!' I waved the handbag. 'This belongs to her.'

'Oh yes,' the female attendant stretched out her hand. I went up the steps into the ambulance to give it to her.

In spite of myself I looked on to the stretcher, thinking to see blood everywhere, a smashed head. The old lady had her eyes closed, the daisy-spattered rainhood still incongruously on her head. She seemed to be sleeping peacefully.

'Is she...?' I said.

'Just a little concussion,' the woman said, 'these wet roads. Is she a relative?'

'A relative?'

They were pulling up the steps at the back of the ambulance.

'Oh no. She dropped her handbag. I was standing next to her. We were waiting to cross the road.'

'Nice of you to come, anyway. She'll be pleased to have someone by her when she comes round.'

It was too fantastic. They were closing the

doors, I moved towards them. The old lady groaned, opened her eyes for a moment and looked at me.

'Lucky the car didn't actually hit her,' the attendant said.

'Didn't it?'

'She just collapsed from fright, thinking it was going to. She hit her head.'

I still had the handbag and turned to lay it on the stretcher.

'Old people all alone,' the woman said, feeling for her pulse, 'they get bewildered in today's traffic. It's hardly surprising.'

'I have to go.'

'We're only taking her to St Patrick's.'

They were bolting the doors.

'I just picked up her handbag.'

'She'll be pleased you did. Probably contains some treasures. We shall be able to find out who she is.'

The ambulance was moving and I sat down with a bump on the stretcher opposite the old lady. The bell began to ring with urgency and I looked out of the blue-smoked windows and wondered what on earth I was doing.

We seemed to be going terribly fast, not stopping for anything. The attendant was a woman in her forties with bell-bottom trousers and old-fashioned, square-shouldered, uniform jacket. From beneath her cap coiled a few grey-blonde curls. She was busy folding blankets and making everything ship-shape. She felt the old lady's pulse very matter-of-factly as if the thin wrist coming out of the raincoat was some inanimate object, a stick or something, which it looked like. I wondered if they ever washed the red blanket and how many babies had been delivered in that confined space and how messy it must get after the really nasty accidents and if that woman, who looked more like a kindly assistant in a grocer's, could really cope. She was talking all the time as she moved; about the fog and the number of accidents it caused and illness among old people. The hospitals were bursting at the seams, she said, with chronic bronchitis. She should really be off duty, was just going off in fact when the call came but her relief hadn't arrived and it was going to make her late but it was just one of those things.

Late! It was ten past two, gone, and Dobbie would be on his second cigarette sure now I wasn't coming. My car was there in the car park, he'd see my car. That was a stoke of luck, putting it there so he must know I intended to be there, would probably wait. I could certainly get a taxi from St Patrick's. People were always coming up to hospitals in taxis, so if I just waited. I looked at the old lady, her wrinkled face serene, her jaw dropped slightly. She didn't have her glasses, perhaps they'd been dropped when she fell, smashed. I wondered whether she could see.

'She was wearing glasses.'

'I have them here. Someone picked them up. Lucky they weren't broken.'

She looked very pale.

'Is she all right?'

'Her pulse is good. They'll X-ray her skull. See if there's any damage. Their bones are brittle. Old people. Here we are.'

She bent her knees to look out of the window. The ambulance made a wide turn and slowed down.

We waited while the driver got out and opened the doors and let down the steps. It was good to breathe the fresh air after the confined space. It hadn't stopped raining but we were under an awning. White paint on the ashphalt where I stepped said 'only'. I presumed we were parked on the bit that said 'ambulances'.

Together the two of them took the stretcher out. They seemed not to have to use a great deal of strength. I was still holding the handbag.

'Can you take this? I have to be off.'

The woman looked round from the hospital entrance which they were half way through with the stretcher.

'Just bring it in will you, dear? We're taking her through to Casualty.'

This was getting ridiculous. I stepped forward to put the handbag on the stretcher so that I could run when a porter said just a moment if you don't mind. I had to stand aside while two stretchers were carried out by white-clad porters. By the time I got inside the doors they were nowhere to be seen with the old lady.

I enquired the way to Casualty and was directed along a tiled corridor like a public lavatory and thought my God English hospitals were the absolute end. We seemed to think of nothing but football pools and cricket and should be filled with shame.

I pushed open the swing doors where it said Casualty and there was a room which seemed to be full of people waiting, a few of them bandaged, a nurse, and some cubicles with green curtains. There was no sign of my two ambulance attendants. The nurse looked harassed and was leaning over a desk writing.

'Can you tell me…?'

'Sit down a moment somewhere will you?' She didn't look up.

'I'm not a patient. They just brought an old lady in, I think it must have been in here. I have her handbag.' I held it up.

She stopped writing. 'Oh yes. Doctor Macintosh is with her now.' She nodded towards one of the cubicles.

'If you could just take this.' I held out the handbag.

With a widening of her eyes she indicated the crowded room, people coming and going, a child crying, the desk on which there wasn't an inch of space, and her own hands which were occupied.

'I have an appointment,' I said weakly.

She looked at my coat with the mink tie and my snake-skin shoes and handbag and stockings Christian Dior, splashed now with mud, and was aware, I knew, of the Memoire Chérie I had dabbed behind my ears and on my brow and dropped in my bra on a piece of cotton wool. There is a life outside I wanted to tell her, but could forgive her, in this atmosphere, for being unaware.

I gave in gracefully. There was no alternative except to hurl the handbag at her and stalk out churlishly. I sat down next to a man holding a filthy handkerchief to his eye. Five minutes would not now make a great deal of difference. As soon as I got rid of the handbag I would phone Dobbie at the flat where he'd most likely go as soon as he got fed up with waiting, to see if I was there.

'The leddy with concussion?' a voice called.

A young man in a white coat with bright red hair sticking up on end stood before me. He looked about nineteen and I presumed it was Doctor Macintosh, doctor, I must be getting old, and he must be more than that.

'Is she all right?'

'Not so bad. Sister will take her particulars and then would you sit beside her and let us know if she comes round? We're short of nurses and the wards are full, no more extra beds after the fog. We'll X-ray for fractures and maybe ye can tek her home.'

'But I'm…' I held up the handbag but he was gone with a swirl of coat behind the curtains of a cubicle.

A Sister with a frilled cap and a nice face had pencil poised.

'You're the lady with the accident? Relative is it?'

'I brought her handbag.'

'May we have her name?'

I explained, slowly, what had happened.

'How kind of you to come. So often these old people have no-one to go home to. Perhaps we shall find some means of identifying her in her handbag.'

I opened it, a reluctant conspirator. The Sister waited, answering countless questions from people who approached her with infinite patience. There was a coloured Woolworth's handkerchief, a pocket comb with two teeth missing, a key, a worn purse which felt as if it had a single coin in it, a pension book.

'Ah!' the Sister said. 'That should tell us.'

I was conscious of my own handbag heavy with the gold compact Tim had bought me, keys and cheque book, in its leather case, wallet with my initials holding driving licence and account cards from Selfridge's and Harrod's, as well as money, and two lipsticks, a Parker Fifty-one with pencil to match and two hankies from the Irish Linen Company.

'Mrs Ellen Potter,' Sister said writing, 'thirteen A, Colchester Street, W6. Date of birth January the seventh 1891.'

It was definitely depressing; the hospital and the people and the man next to me with his grubby handkerchief; most of all Ellen Potter with her plastic head-gear, old as time.

'You're going to be kind enough to sit with her, Doctor Macintosh said.'

I nodded.

'It's like a mad house today after the fog.' She handed me the pension book which I put back into the handbag of which I seemed unable to rid myself.

'I have to make a telephone call.'

Three

I dialled the number picturing Dobbie having gone home wondering what had happened to me. Then I looked at my watch and it was still only 2.30 so if he had given up the wait he would probably still be in the traffic somewhere en route. I let it ring and ring and ring to the empty flat, which should have been witnessing scenes of passion, then replaced the receiver slowly.

The telephone booth was in the main hall. Outside it people were coming and going with purpose or sitting passively on the benches. I walked across the black and white floor towards the Casualty department then thought how utterly ridiculous. There was no need to go back in there at all. I owed nothing, nothing at all to Ellen Potter. She would be quite adequately looked after, these accidents happened every moment of the day, and I could walk right out, pick up a taxi and go straight to Dobbie's, be there waiting for him. I had after all promised and he had kept the afternoon free. Stupid really to have arranged to meet him at the car park. I made up my mind, redid the mink tie which had come loose round the collar of my coat, and hurried towards the main doors. Something flapped against my side. It was Ellen Potter's handbag; also I had left the red umbrella in the Casualty department. There was a dreamlike quality in the brown plastic handbag of which I seemed unable to rid myself, the edifice around me of the hospital. In my snakeskin shoes I did not belong. Why was I here in the middle of the afternoon when I should have been making love with Dobbie? I could give the handbag to one of the porters; there was still the umbrella. I couldn't send him in for that. It wasn't an hotel. Half an hour then. I had after all promised. I would do the stint with the old lady then ring Dobbie again.

They had taken off her navy blue mac. She was wearing a print dress unsuitable for November and a hand-knitted cardigan. The inevitable red blanket was over her but her hands were on top of it twisted a little with rheumatism and desperately plain. She was still sleeping and I wondered if there was anyone to care. Had it been me Tim would have been there fussing about private rooms and specialists and Martha and my mother from Sussex. There was a chair by the curtain and I moved it a little nearer to the bed. The legs made a squeaking noise on the floor and the old lady opened her eyes and looked at me.

'Jean. Is that you Jean?'

'No. I'm afraid it isn't.'

'Of course not. Jean's dead.'

She shut her eyes again and I wondered who Jean was and whether I should call someone.

'Is there someone I could get in touch with?' I said. 'Tell them you've had an accident.'

There was no response. It was twenty to three. I thought of Dobbie. The old story came into my head about the butterfly and I wondered whether I was really sitting here in the Casualty department of St Patrick's hospital imagining I was with Dobbie or whether I was in fact with Dobbie and dreaming myself beside Ellen Potter of whose existence I had been unaware until less than an hour ago. The child waiting to be seen by Doctor Macintosh was still crying. Shutting my ears to the sound I returned in the rain to Orchard Street; a butterfly dreaming I was a man. Next to the lady in the plastic rain-hat I waited to cross the road. The lights changed from red to amber, green. In a posse we charged heads down. The old lady disappeared in the direction of Marble Arch.

'You're late,' Dobbie said. 'I was getting worried.'

I slid in beside him. 'I had lunch with Martha. I couldn't get a taxi.'

Tim would have said you're all right? You're sure you're all right?

227

Dobbie put the red umbrella at the back.

'I had to buy it,' I said nervously. 'I didn't know it was going to rain.'

He turned the key in the ignition. 'Better than that damned fog.'

No kiss; talking about the weather like … anybody.

He put a hand on my knee. 'Don't look so worried.'

'I'm not. Just harrassed. I had to rush.'

'Calm down. You're here now. Nothing to worry about.' He looked as he did any other day; unperturbed.

'I wonder when it will stop?'

'What?' He looked at me.

'The rain.'

He laughed.

'What's funny?'

'You are nervous.'

'It's the first time for me.'

'Now now!'

'Sorry. I can't help thinking of Catherine, all those beautiful girls who spend days in the hairdresser's, hours putting their faces on.'

He laughed again.

'Don't pretend you like us *au naturel*. Most of us look ghastly.'

'You all look the same in the dark.'

'Don't tease.'

In the dark. I wondered if Dobbie liked to make love with the light on. Of course it was

228

the middle of the afternoon so there wasn't much choice. Not unless you deliberately drew the curtains. The question wouldn't arise.

In the flat I thought this is it. No turning back now. Dobbie took my coat which was damp and put it on a hanger to dry. I put my gloves and the mink tie on the table folding them with unnecessary precision.

'Like a drink?' True to film prototype he held the bottle questioningly.

'Please.' Perhaps I'd feel less nervous.

He poured one each.

'Cheers.'

'Cheers.'

I made mine last. Dobbie finished his and looked at me.

'What time have you to be back?'

'For the children at four.'

He looked at his watch. 'Plenty of time.'

I wished he hadn't said that, it seemed so calculating, five minutes for drinks, five minutes' chat, etc., etc.

He took the glass from my hand. 'You don't really want that.'

'No.'

He put his arms round me. I felt all the tension slipping away. Thoughts of home and the children and Martha and the rain and being late for Dobbie. He kissed me and I responded as if it wasn't me, Liz Westbury, at all but Cleopatra and Madame de Pompa-

229

dour and Lady Hamilton and all women through the ages become one; living only for the gratification of self and man. I no longer knew who or where or when only that for the first time in my life nothing mattered. Nothing was important. I was amoeba flowing in all directions, formless without purpose. I was meaningless except as I concerned my mate, part of a living, striving thing, seeking together something which was reality and which was not. I did not know whether the light was on or off nor where my clothes went to and how nor the duration, nor the attitude struck. Only that the climax of the encounter was a sinking into a dark chasm, a floating ball of fire, a consummation. Only slowly, a drifting to the surface through quiet seas, did reality return.

'I thought you were Jean,' a voice said.

With a shock I realised where I was and that the woman in the bed was talking to me.

I was angry with her for disturbing my moments with Dobbie.

'It's not having my glasses. I suppose you don't know what they've done with my glasses.'

'I'm afraid I don't.'

'Silly anyway. Jean's dead. You get confused.'

I willed her to go back to sleep or whatever it was. As if in obedience she closed her eyes.

I was in Dobbie's bed. Dobbie was smoking. There were clothes all over the floor. I had done it. Committed adultery. I did not feel particularly wicked.

'I have to make a phone call,' Dobbie said and dialled a number with the hand that held the cigarette. I wondered whether I had been all right and thought that I must have been.

He spoke to his secretary and gave her various instructions about whom she should phone. He said he'd be at the flat for another half an hour if she wanted him. Half an hour. Suppose I refused to go.

'What is the time?'

'Four.'

'What?'

'Four o'clock.'

'You're joking.'

He showed me his watch. There were black hairs on his wrist.

I struggled up. 'The children.'

'Take it easy. I'll run you back to the car park. I envy Tim.'

I wasn't like that with Tim. Not often these days anyway. There was too much intervening, children, plans, money. I didn't disillusion him.

'You know something, Liz?'

'Mm?'

'Suppose you didn't go home.'

I stretched out again. 'That would be nice.'

He stubbed out his cigarette and rolled on to me. Twice in one afternoon. It hadn't happened since my honeymoon.

Ellen Potter's eyes were on me.

'You wouldn't happen to know what I'm doing here?'

I forced my mind back. 'There was an accident, in Orchard Street. You were waiting to cross the road.'

'Did I hurt myself?'

'I don't think so. Just bumped your head. The car didn't actually hit you.'

She put a hand to her head and sat up.

'Well if I'm all right I suppose I can go home. There's no point in lying here.'

'I'll call somebody. I was staying with you until you felt better. I believe they want to X-ray your skull.'

'What for?'

'To see if there's any damage.'

'I don't believe in X-rays. They're radio-active.'

'I'll tell Sister you're feeling better anyway.'

I beckoned Sister from the cubicle. She came, smiling sweetly, and said: 'Feeling better, Mrs Potter? That's right. You're going up to X-ray now just to make certain there's no damage done.'

'It's only a bump,' the old lady said. 'I'd better be getting home. I don't like being out in the dark.'

'We shan't keep you very long.'

'Sister!' a voice called.

'I'm coming, Doctor Macintosh.'

Two porters, spotty youths in hospital caps and gowns came to carry her away. She was still protesting about the X-ray and that she was perfectly all right, no bones broken. I was left alone with the navy raincoat, two handbags, and the red umbrella.

I went to phone Dobbie again but still there was no reply. It was a quarter-past three and unlikely that he would have waited at the car park for so long. If he hadn't gone back to the flat where was he? Moved on perhaps to his next engagement. I let it ring a little longer. He was coming now, his key already in the door. Even if he was it was too late. I had to get back for the children. Too late. I hung up, shutting off the monotonous sound. I could turn my attentions to Ellen Potter. Ellen Potter. If I went now, just left, they would send her home by ambulance presuming she was all right, no bones broken. I was no longer in any rush, and decided to act like a lady. Like a lady, ha! That was funny. The afternoon had turned out to be quite different to expectation. I wondered where Dobbie was and if he was disappointed.

Back in the cubicle, which was still empty, I sat down once more to wait and thought how easily, another moment, snuff, Ellen

Potter might have died, splashed by the rain, in Orchard Street.

I was afraid of death and was glad I hadn't had to look at it. It wasn't the actual dying, of course, that was easy enough requiring no effort on one's behalf like being born. It was the thought of obliteration that was difficult to stomach. A world without one's own presence; the unsavoury thought that life could go on callously unchanged, whether you were there or not. You wanted to be there, if only as a fly on the wall, to hear them say poor Liz, watch their tears as they attempted pathetically to fill the gap you had left.

How must it be to be Ellen Potter? To look in the mirror, see the muscles sagging that once had been so firm, the hair, no pigment left of youth, teeth no longer your own. Could life be bearable when you knew it could not be for long? Did anyone leave willingly, without protest? Whichever way you turned, surely there was death. You watched the leaves curl and drop in autumn, the flower-decked hearse as you crossed the street, the back page of the newspaper, and knew there was no escape. I wondered, when it came to my turn whether I could go about my daily business, waiting philosophically for death, or if I would scream like a child protesting at the dark, go mad, rebel. No-one ever did. Tim said people who were afraid to die were afraid to live. I'm sure he was right. Those who lived life to the full, climbed mountains, explored the deep, tested jets, shrugged their shoulders at disaster; if they thought of it at all.

Reflecting on Tim I thought what a joke really. I will come home to you faithful after all. It would only be a question of time because I would arrange to meet Dobbie again, perhaps tomorrow. Tomorrow was my committee afternoon. I had been talked into the Vice Presidency because no-one else would accept the office. I was expected to be there, at the top table, at every meeting. If Dobbie was free, they would just have to do without me. 'Where's Liz today?' they'd say. I pictured the expression on their faces if they knew, sitting there in their best hats for the most part expensive but not chic. None of us were really chic. In our brave attempts to be we envied the slim hips or hiplessness of the eighteen-year-olds, and quarrelled about the organisation of the organisation. We became so involved sometimes with internal strife, conflict over who should run the tombola for our dance, whose teenage daughter should sell programmes at the theatre we had hired, we were apt to lose sight of the various needs which from our general purposes committee we supported. Often I sat doodling on the paper the committee was supplied with, or taking sips from the glass of water, and listened to Olga, or one of the others, arguing about which one of us should approach to a certain big business firm for gifts for our Christmas bazaar, and wondered what it really had to do with the limbless children for whom we were collecting. The really stupid part about it all, us losing sight of our cause, I mean, came when a benefactor with friends on two committees gave a donation to a society other than our own. We were up in arms. We had our target to reach. Feuds arose in which we almost but not quite reached for each other's tinted hair. We forgot that the fund would benefit through whichever channel the donation reached it. We did our best. We were neither Doctor Schweitzers nor Edith Cavells. If our Coffee Mornings, our Bridge Afternoons which turned into cake-making contests, the eaters protesting, all on diets, were so much time wasted, they were time wasted in a good cause. We tried to help. Ultimately we did; just went about it in rather a roundabout way. From our hot-beds of gossip sprang clothing and money for earthquake victims. From an evening of dining and dancing in which our own bellies, true, were filled too full, a morsel of food for the starving half of the world. Tomorrow they would manage without me. The meet-ing was at Martha's and concerned the Ball we were holding after Christmas. Exactly as much would be achieved without me and could be achieved without half the people there. There was a handful who really did the work and a dozen others who drifted along not raising their voices except parrot-like to agree or disagree. Where's Liz? Committing adultery. Really? How nice. Yes perhaps I will have another teeny-weeny piece of that cheese cake.

Four

It was quiet now in the green-curtained cubicle; impersonal. Patients would come and go, leaving nothing, no evidence that they had been. The chair was hard. I wondered how much of the afternoon Dobbie had spent waiting for me in the rain; how much of his time I was worth. Conjuring him up into almost flesh and blood, the cynical blue eyes which 'sent me' as Diana would say, I tried to analyse my motives for wanting him. It wasn't as if I had an unsatisfactory love-life with Tim. No that wasn't strictly honest, how rarely one was with oneself. So stupid, there was no-one else around yet you duped, prevaricated, until you measured up to your own standards. I came to my marriage a virgin. Most of us did, not like today. It was the rule, not the exception.

When I got engaged to Tim in the village in the rain I was seventeen. I was eighteen and the war over before I saw him again. After he'd left for his unknown destination there were three letters. I had them still in a locked drawer together with Diana's first blonde curl and some poetry I wrote when they sent the telegram to say Tim was missing. Our marriage was to be the marriage of them all. The three letters were Tim's ideas of how it was going to be. They spoke for the most part of sensual pleasures. Neither of us visualised the long night ending; that afterwards would come the hard part of living near each other, for each other. It was like an examination in which you were confident of your success yet had no idea of the syllabus. Perhaps it was just as well.

When Tim came back from the prisoner-of-war camp they took him straight to hospital. I didn't recognise him. The love I had been fostering was not for this wreck of a human being. I tried not to let him see.

I had scrounged clothing coupons from everyone for this moment and had on a new dress with a matching coat. I put on a bright smile.

'You look wonderful, Liz.'

'What was it like?'

'A piece of cake.' The grin consumed his face without disturbing the eyes.

'No, really.'

'Lonely. That was the worst part.'

He couldn't have weighed more than six stone. It did not look like the worst.

'Some days I really thought the war would end and we'd be married. Those were the good ones.'

'And on the bad?' I wanted to keep him talking about himself.

'On the bad days I wallowed in self-pity. I knew I'd never come back; never. Men would be born with nose, eyes, mouth, forehead, and a soul like mine but my thoughts, hopes, dreams, ambitions, would never be repeated. The world could go on for a million trillion years and I would never be seen again. Stupid, wasn't it?'

'No.'

'I felt hell's sorry for myself. I wanted someone to love me, help me. We couldn't help each other and no-one else would come. Some of the boys just died quietly, because of that. They had nothing to hold on to. I had you. Let's get married soon. I don't want to be alone any more.'

It was the only time he spoke of it and I wanted to cry. Not only for Tim but the whole of humanity kicking stones behind barbed wire, waiting to be rescued. I sat on my chair by the bed smiling brightly and feeling, other than disgust for the pitted skin, the skeletal hand on the sheet, nothing; nothing at all.

While Tim came slowly back to life I went out with a boy called Edgar. My war had been spent in a village; Tim was its aftermath and I could not face it. The war had nothing to do with Edgar except that it had made him rich. We moved back to town. Our house had been gutted by incendiaries so we took a flat. Edgar had the flat next door. He was very smooth, not bad-looking and always wore a red carnation. He had a car when few people had and no difficulty with petrol. When we met downstairs he'd give me a lift to the hospital to see Tim. One day he waited and took me out to dinner. Steaks, the size of the plate, appeared by magic, lashings of butter; we danced. He wore a gold ring on his little finger and called me Elizabeth. My days were divided between Tim and Edgar. I could bear it in the hospital with its sickening smell and its insularity because downstairs Edgar would be waiting.

Sometimes I worried at my own indifference. They were a pathetic lot in Tim's ward, bandaged, emaciated, shuffling in dressing-gowns or in bed. I should have loved them all, Tim in particular. I watched the other women, wives, sweethearts, and hated myself for my false smile, brittle laughter, waiting to get back to Edgar.

It took Tim all winter to creep back to health. One freak day in February the temperature climbed to the middle sixties. A warm sun shone on the naked trees. Tim's bed was empty and his wheel-chair gone. Through the French windows at the end of the ward I could see a gouache of hospital blue on the balcony.

'Looking for Tim?' someone said. 'Over there.'

In his ill-fitting blues he was leaning over the balustrade looking out into the gardens. There was nothing much to see except a patch of lawn and some laurel bushes. To Tim I suppose they looked good. He had regained most of his weight and was almost like the Tim of two years ago. It was the first time I had seen him on his feet. I leaned on the rail next to him not sure if he had seen me. He seemed to be miles away. After a while he said, 'It will soon be spring.' I knew he meant that he would be free to enjoy it. In the forecourt I could just see Edgar's car.

It was very warm, almost like summer. I had on a suit and a heavy coat on top. I started to take off the coat and Tim turned to help me.

'I can manage.' I turned away to take my arms out of the sleeves, then back towards him. Perhaps it was the first time I'd really looked at him; perhaps I was off guard, not tense with fear at what I might find in his face. He stood there holding the coat, with its utility label in the lining, smiling a little, and in that moment everything came ricocheting back, love, desire, the lot. I wanted to kiss him, to bury myself in his face.

He put the coat on the coping between us and we looked again at the garden. We didn't speak for a long while then Tim said: 'Bit dicey for a while wasn't it, Liz?'

I'd tried so hard not to let him know.

'Who's the type with the Humber and the red carnation?'

I didn't answer and he said: 'I guessed there was someone. Shorty used to give me the gen.'

'His name's Edgar. I'm sorry.'

'There's nothing to be sorry about.'

I worried. What sort of a love was it that couldn't face what I'd had to face with Tim? That fled in the face of adversity. I wrote a letter to Edgar and put it through the door of his flat. Tim was moved to a convalescent home in the country. We walked in the burgeoning countryside and it was he who consoled me as if I had suffered.

'It was a shock, Liz. You weren't prepared.'

'I'd seen pictures.'

'Not of people you loved.'

'Where was my compassion?'

'You were a kid; scared stiff. I watched you.'

'I feel so ashamed.'

'I wasn't worried. I knew you'd come back.'

'How?'

'Because I love you. I've always loved you. Always will. Always.'

Always.

This was the man I was planning to deceive.

After he was demobbed … nothing remaining, externally at any rate, of what he had been through, Tim had to study for his accountancy exams. He had a small income from some money his grandfather had left him, his gratuity and the back pay from the years in captivity. We found a tiny flat and sent out the wedding invitations.

At the ceremony the 'boys', those that were left, formed a guard of honour. At the reception they got high and maudlin at their own rendering of *Nellie Dean*.

We went to Cornwall for our honeymoon. The highlight was waking the first morning with Tim in the same bed. A sensual perfection matched by only one other. The moment after giving birth to Diana without benefit of anaesthetic; an instant when you knew the beauty of the whole world. Honeymoons they say often go wrong. Ours didn't. We expiated our loneliness in a world where no-one understood us completely. Tim's degrading years as a prisoner, our youth. We knew the day would never come when we could be in a room together without touching, within sight without feeling the demands of the flesh.

We settled to life in our little flat. Tim studying, me working part-time, cooking, housekeeping, both of us willing at any time to stop what we were doing to make love. One night Tim woke me up screaming obscenities and beating his pillow. I put on the light, frightened, and called to him but he didn't seem to hear, I touched him but he flailed at me with his arms. Tim, I kept calling, Tim. Suddenly, with no warning he quietened down and turning over on his side went to sleep.

In the morning he said he didn't remember dreaming, certainly not attacking anyone. I was afraid, thinking the pillow might one night be me. The attacks became a regular occurrence, happening once or twice a month. Sometimes he spoke coherently about bailing out and the kite being on fire and bloody Nips and filthy bastards. In the morning he never remembered. I talked about it to a doctor who said the war didn't end when it stopped and advised me to get single beds. I didn't take his advice. Gradually the incidents became less frequent. There was never any warning of when they would come and they never failed to terrify me. When I asked him what it was like in the camp he said boring mostly but a guarded look would come into his eyes and I could see that he was remembering, reliving things, things he would never forget, of which I would never have any part.

The double bed helped us over our first quarrel. I can't remember what it was about other than it was not a major issue; they rarely are. Most likely it was a wrong word said at an inopportune moment and touching a raw nerve. I don't know. If the first act was hazy the last stuck in my mind. Perhaps because I used physical violence; I was young enough for that.

It started I believe in our kitchen, which was no bigger than a cupboard, just as we were going to bed. In no time at all the scene had shifted to the bedroom where we un-dressed coldly hurling insults at each other.

Tim belittled my mother, I retaliated with his Uncle Alfred of whom he thought the world. I called him brutal. He said I was immature. I sniffed 'where there's no sense there's no feeling'. He thought it was time I grew up. I said I should never have married him. He buttoned his pyjama jacket and said nobody else had asked me. It was true and I saw red. I called him a liar, there had been all kinds of people while he was away. He challenged me to name them. I was hopping mad. He said I was jolly lucky he'd asked me. I picked up my slipper and let go. It had a wedge heel and nicked his shoulder and shattered the mirror behind him. You might have killed me, he said and climbed with dignity into bed. I will next time. He turned over. Don't wake me up. In the bath-room I looked with pity at my tear-streaked face, dishevelled hair, wondered if I could get a divorce for cruelty, what my mother would say when she saw me on her doorstep with my case.

I climbed into bed carefully keeping to my

own side, making sure I didn't come into contact with Tim. Never sleep on a quarrel had been a nursery maxim. Neither would we if Tim would apologise. He was breathing steadily.

'You might at least say sorry.'

No reply. I was sure he wasn't really asleep.

'Tim, did you hear me?'

'I did and I think you've a bloody nerve. You might have killed me with that thing.'

'Well I didn't.'

'Thanks.'

'Anyway look at the things you said about my mother.'

'To pay you back for Uncle Alfred.'

'That was before.'

'It wasn't it was after.'

'You said...'

'*You* said...'

'You started the whole thing.'

'*I* did? I like that. *You* said ... and *I* said...'

I don't remember the outcome of round two. Only that it was after midnight and we were both exhausted and muddled with reiteration and hardly able to recall what it had all been about ourselves. There was an oasis of silence after we'd said a chilly 'good night then' and agreed to go to sleep. We both had to work in the morning. In single beds most likely it would have ended there. In the one we shared it was Tim's toe, my leg, his arm, my shoulder, his thigh and mine, our bodies indistinguishable, confused, fused one with the other protesting our love.

There were quarrels after, not of the same caliber. I never again resorted to physical violence, had to explain away a broken mirror. I suppose we both grew more tolerant, diplomatic, rubbed down the first uneven edges of our marriage. Looking back to the little flat, the smithereens of glass lying like glittering object lessons on the floor, it seemed fun, the turbulence to which we could be stirred. Perhaps we had lost something.

We'd gained stability. The end of that first hectic period came when I passed out queuing for chocolate biscuits (postscript to a war which had ended five years before) in the Home & Colonial and we knew Diana was on the way.

After that things moved fast. Tim qualified and we put the money down for our house in the village. In the first months of pregnancy I felt myself an object of the utmost interest, and it was a time, apart from the minor discomforts, of great contentment. Diana was born after a cold, wet, lonely and miserable night in the labour ward, at six o'clock in the morning. After the single moment of intense joy which followed her birth and my happiness with Tim when suddenly we were three there was no peace. I was busy with meals and beds and drinks and feeds when all I craved was sleep. The horrid memories of that birth stayed with me for two years and I booked to have Robin in a private nursing home where funnily enough the patient was important. I settled at the end for oblivion and forewent my crest of achievement.

It took time to adjust to the new pattern. Instead of just Tim I had Diana too; at six in the morning and at ten at night; often in between in the small hours, in which I never got used to leaving my bed. When Tim wanted to make love I was submissive; sometimes, despite myself, not even that. There was no-one to tell us that after a birth it was normal. We recaptured the old days on a Mediterranean holiday, Diana with Grandma, then we started again with Robin and it was as if we had always been four.

There began to be problems. They had to do with being tired at the end of the day, a toddler and meals and a biggish house, help once a week then, the irksomeness of contraceptive devices and a baby. Sometimes I felt like making love in the middle of the day; after lunch when the children were resting, only of course Tim wasn't there. He was very patient.

There were bad patches, then as the children grew, peace. Out of the chaos a pattern emerged. I suspected it prevailed in the village. Sometimes I discussed it with Martha. It was a swinging graft with moments of despair and others of content during which you imagined the old spontaneity hadn't quite gone. Tim said I was prettier than all the girls on the Italian beaches. He meant it too, faithful and loving I knew, yet he looked at them wondering what he was missing, bored with the old routine. There were too many factors, hair-do's and what you had to do next day and the children might come in, they threw a pall of reserve giving birth to the village neuroses of which I too was victim. In our dreams we were wild, wicked, abandoned. We wanted lovers; we had husbands. I wanted both. Dobbie too. Anyone. It didn't matter.

Five

It was half-past three when they brought her back. Doctor Macintosh came with her.

'No damage done,' he said. 'A night's sleep and she'll be hopping around like a two-year-old.' He laid a freckled hand on the old lady's knotted one for a moment, young enough to be her grandson. It was Christ healing the lepers, making the dumb man speak. You could see he didn't mind, however old, however dirty. Only the insincere would bother him, the malingerers, the *poseurs*. His expression was distant when he turned to me. 'Keep an eye on her for twenty-four hours,' he said and was gone. Sister who was with him stayed to help her up and with her coat, fastening it for her like a child.

The crowd in the casualty room had thinned. The man with the grubby handkerchief had gone. I felt as if I had been there all day. Outside the rain had stopped, leaving great puddles in the forecourt. Mrs Potter looked about.

'I wonder where we are,' she said. 'I can get a seventy-four from Marble Arch.' She looked at her watch, held it to her ear, shook

251

it. 'Oh dear, it's stopped. I hope it's not broken.'

She seemed more anxious about it than she was about her fall. It was a cheap little watch on a black ribbon.

'You probably knocked it as you fell. They'll be able to repair it. If we can get a taxi to where I've let my car I'll take you home.'

'It's very kind of you but please don't worry about me. If you can just tell me where we are I can get on a bus.'

A taxi swung into the yard and a young man in a bowler hat, holding a bunch of red roses awkwardly got out.

I took her arm. 'We'll take this.'

'If you'd like to drop me off at the bus then.'

I helped her in and told the driver to take us to the car park.

'Have you the time?'

I looked at my watch, oblong-faced on a gold bracelet, an anniversary present from Tim. 'It's nearly four. Look, if you don't mind I'll take you home with me first because the children will be in. We could have a cup of tea then I'll run you home afterwards.'

'I really don't want to put you to any trouble. I don't even know your name.'

'I'm Mrs Westbury.'

'Mine's Potter. Ellen Potter.'

'Who's Jean?'

'Jean?'

'You were talking about her. You thought I was her.'

'She was a little like you, tall and slim. My husband was very tall.'

'Your daughter?'

'Yes.'

'Where is she?'

'She's dead. A growth. Two years ago.'

'The only one?'

'Only girl. I had two boys. I lost one as a baby with enteritis and the other boy at Arnhem. He was a paratrooper. We went to see his grave. My husband died last year. He had lung trouble ever since the First World War.'

She was peering out of the window. 'Are we anywhere near the Edgware Road?'

'Look, please don't worry. I'll see that you get home.'

She shook her watch and held it to her ear.

'Are you feeling all right?'

'Quite thank you. I suppose I fell on it.' She was still worried about the watch.

'It's probably quite a minor thing. I shouldn't worry.'

I tapped on the driver's glass window. 'Thank you. You can drop us here.'

I looked quickly round the two brick-walled sides of the bomb-site, stupidly, for Dobbie. I hadn't really expected him to wait two hours; it seemed more like ten.

There was a note, sopping wet on the windscreen, beneath the wiper. I opened it but the ink had run into great blue tears. I couldn't read a single word. I blinked, frustrated, in an attempt to get them into focus but of course it was useless. I pictured Dobbie writing it, 'Darling, I love you, what happened?' 'Darling Liz I waited all the afternoon.' It was only blotches of washable blue like Rorschach's test for assessing your personality.

'Is anything wrong?' Ellen said.

I had forgotten about her.

'No, nothing.'

I found my keys and unlocked the car. She sat very neatly next to me.

'It's the first time I've been in a car.'

It had never occurred to me that there were people who had never been in a car.

'It's a lovely car. George was keen on cars. He had a motorbike.'

'George was the paratrooper?'

'Yes. I like walking. I do a lot of walking. Will they be waiting for their tea?'

'Who?'

'Your children.'

'No. We'll be in time. Robin has the key anyway but I like to be there.'

'Cook their own do they?'

'Cook? No. They help themselves to biscuits and milk or raid the fridge for leftovers. We have dinner fairly early.'

'How old are they?'

'Robin's ten and Diana twelve.'

'You look very young. I wish I hadn't broken my watch.'

We were out of the traffic now and into the suburbs. Stupidly I had palpitations wondering if Dobbie was waiting for me at home.

There was no Mercedes in the road, green or otherwise. Perhaps he had telephoned getting no reply.

'This is where I live.'

'What a lovely house.'

Medium nice. I'd always had a yen for a town house. I didn't mind about the number of storeys or a basement, in Lowndes Square or Cheyne Walk or else by the river or in the country in its own acres with lawns and flowerbeds where you could lose yourself.

We stopped in the drive. 'If you get out I'll lock it after you.'

She looked at the door handle, the window winder, the ashtray, fingering them nervously.

'It's that one. Pull it towards you.'

She held it uncertainly.

'Wait there. I'll do it.'

I opened the door and she got out clumsily, looking at the house with its pine front door and draped curtains.

'I'll just see if the children are in then I'll come back for the shopping.'

Mrs Mac had left the house tidy. There

was an advert for soap powder stuck through the letter box. It felt unoccupied.

'Robin! Di!' I waited. 'They aren't home.'

I took the shopping basket out of the boot.

'What about this?' Ellen Potter said. 'Shall I bring it?'

It was Diana's skirt, I'd forgotten to take it to the cleaner's.

'No. I'll take it tomorrow.' Another of the things I had planned to do and hadn't.

In the kitchen I said, 'I expect you could do with a cup of tea.'

'I'm being such a nuisance.'

'I'm gasping anyway.'

I put the kettle on and took her coat and showed her where to wash. In the kitchen I let down the Venetian blinds, the slats open, and switched on the fluorescent light waiting for it to pop-pop into life.

When she came back I was getting the stewing steak I had got from the supermarket what seemed years ago ready for the pressure cooker.

She sat stiffly on the grey, plastic-topped stool, and looked around.

'It's a lovely kitchen.'

'Yes.'

'All electric. I'm a little bit afraid of electricity.'

'The machines look a bit fearsome but you soon get used to them. They make life easier. Especially with a family.'

I gave her her tea and thought perhaps I'd said the wrong thing about a family remembering what had happened to hers.

'Don't they cost a terrible lot though?'

'They do, yes.' The new kitchen two years ago had cost Tim eight hundred pounds.

'Everything goes up and up except our pension. I don't know what I'm going to do about coal this winter.'

The pressure cooker was hissing and I turned the heat down and unwrapped the frozen pastry.

'It looks as if we're going to get a Labour Government too.'

'Don't you want one?' I was surprised.

'I don't, no. I've always voted Conservative, my husband too. Not that it's the same without Churchill. You always felt, when you heard him on the radio, that everything was going to be all right. I won't say a lot hasn't been done in my lifetime, well since the war really, milk for the kiddies and school dinners and the National Health but there's a lot more needs doing. Of course they have to spend a good bit on these bombs, but you can't really grudge that.'

I rolled the pastry.

'You aren't a ban-the-bomber then?'

'I think it's scandalous. These bits of boys and girls who go along to make an exhibition of themselves and even the clergy getting mixed up in it. After all it's for our own protection.'

'Or destruction.'

'I've seen people march for all sorts of things in my time. Sit down, stand up, wave banners. It never does a mite of good. Most of them don't know what they're marching for anyway. If there was a march in the other direction they'd join that too. Does that pastry come all ready?'

'Quick-frozen, yes.'

'Marvellous, isn't it. My husband used to like pastry. Of course when you're on your own you don't bother.'

'Would you like another cup of tea?'

'If there's one in the pot. Let me get it. I'm not used to sitting.'

'Are you feeling all right?'

'Yes thanks.' She felt the side of her head. 'I must have a bruise coming.'

'Will they be worrying about you?'

'Who?'

'At home.'

'There's no-one to worry.'

'You live on your own?'

'I've got used to it,' she said defensively.

'They said you had to be looked after.'

'I can look after myself. Have you any idea of the time? I don't like being out in the dark.'

I struggled with my conscience.

'Look, you'd better stay here for tonight.'

'I've given you quite enough trouble

258

already. I really have to get home.'

'But there's no-one there.' No-one to care, but I didn't say it.

'I don't like being out in the dark. I took the bus as far as Piccadilly then walked down Regent Street and along towards Marble Arch. I like looking in the shops when it's getting near Christmas.' She looked at the broken watch.

'It's half-past four.'

She stood up and carried our two cups over to the sink turning the water.

'Leave them. They go in the dishwasher with the dinner dishes.'

'It won't take a moment.'

I let her wash them, picturing her at home alone passing out with concussion or whatever one did.

'You must stay. Just for tonight. I promised the doctor you wouldn't be alone. We've a spare bedroom.'

The bed was not made up. Had I known Mrs Mac could have done it before she went home.

She went out into the hall and came back with her coat on.

'I can't allow you to go.'

She fastened the buckle. 'There's Ginger anyway.'

'Ginger?'

'My cat. He'll be waiting to go out.' She sat down suddenly on the stool.

'What's the matter?'

'Funny. Everything went round suddenly.'

'You see.'

She put her head down.

'Please come upstairs and lie down.'

The back door opened and Robin and Diana came in.

'Hello, Mum!'

'I got a star for History...'

They stared at Ellen Potter.

I helped her up. 'I'll be back in a moment. Take some tea.'

Upstairs she said, 'What about Ginger?'

'Can't I telephone a neighbour to let him out?'

She looked at me. 'There's no telephone.'

I took off her coat again and could see that she was glad to lie down on the spare-room bed.

'I'll be all right in a moment. Must be this wretched bump.'

'Would you like a little brandy?'

She shook her head.

'I'll tell you what. As soon as I've got the dinner ready I'll pop over and let Ginger out. Diana can manage.'

'Oh no, please...'

'I insist. You aren't in a fit state...'

'I'd rather you didn't...' she looked quite distressed.

'He has to be let out hasn't he? Besides I could bring your things.'

She looked at me oddly.

'If you give me your key I can go without disturbing you. Perhaps you'll sleep. It's Colchester Street, isn't it?'

'It's not very easy to find. You want Fulham Palace Road, Wargrave Road, left into Hawtry Street and Gorringe Place; Colchester Street is the third on the left. There's a scrap-iron on the corner.'

'Don't worry. I've a street map. I have to have. No sense of direction.'

'I'd rather go home if my head would stop spinning.'

'I'm sure you would but it wouldn't be wise. What do I do with Ginger? Just let him out?'

'I'm sorry to put you to so much bother.'

'Not trouble at all,' I lied, not feeling in the least like driving to Fulham. 'Is there anything else you want?'

'It will go off in a moment.'

'From home I meant.'

'No, thank you.'

'Robin and Diana are downstairs and my husband will be home shortly if you need anything.'

She shut her eyes. I put the raincoat over the chair and left leaving the door ajar.

'Who was that?' Diana said.

'A lady who had a street accident. She isn't feeling very well.'

'What's she come here for?'

'I was going to take her home but there's no-one to look after her. She's going to stay the night.'

'What did she hurt?' Robin said.

'Nothing really. Just bumped her head.'

He looked disappointed.

'May I go and play with Jane?' Diana said.

'No you'll have to stay here and see to dinner while I go over and let Mrs Potter's cat out.'

'Can I come with you?' Robin said.

'Better stay with Diana. In case Mrs Potter needs anything.'

'Can you make me a monkey's dress for Friday?' Diana said.

'What on earth for?'

'We're doing a play in French. I'm the monkey.'

'You don't need to dress up,' Robin said.

'Couldn't you have picked something less complicated?'

'It's the best part.'

'You've split your blouse,' Robin said. 'Under the arm.'

Diana raised her arm to look, examining her shirt with the other hand.

'Look at the monkey scratching!'

'I suppose you think that's clever.'

'Very.'

'Look, out of the kitchen if you can't stop squabbling!'

'Well can I go to Jane's?'

'No.'

She held her hair up on top of her head. 'Does it suit me like this?'

'Quite.' I went closer. 'Did you wash your neck last night?'

She let the hair flop down.

I finished the steak pie.

'Tell Daddy about Mrs Potter and put this in the oven and the potatoes on at half-past. I shouldn't be long but there'll be all the traffic now.'

'What's for afters?'

'Peaches.'

'Pineapple,' Robin said.

'Whatever you like. You can open it.'

'We had peaches for lunch.'

'Lucky beggar,' Robin said. 'We had stodge.'

Six

The roads were still wet and the evening traffic beginning to build up in the gloom that threatened more fog. At the wheels of Fords and Renaults, Rovers and Jags, men drove with gritted teeth, cut in, overtook at every opportunity, concerned with knocking minutes off the journey. Night and morning a madness gripped them. They were not to blame. Roads filled to more than capacity frustrated them twice in twelve hours. The alternative was the tube, strap-hanging, hemmed in by stale breath, or queueing for buses. They regarded each setback as a personal affront, unlike women were unable to sit back, allow the situation to flow over them. Possessed by devils, like knights of old, they had to beat the lights, the car in front; had to. We were more equable, better able to cope. We had to be. We had, in addition, our bodies to deal with. What did men know of fortitude? They were the bead-winners, yes, struggled for their living, ours. Each day though was the same. Their prowess was governed by intellectual or manual ability; ours by hormones. Some mornings we woke up ten feet tall, on others devoid of strength enough to pluck our eyebrows. One week found us moving mountains, on our knees cleaning loft or garage, the next incapable of throwing away the things on saucers that had accumulated in the fridge. How would men like, in addition to their daily round, the insufferable worry of every month? The days, which seemed a life-time long, when you were unsure whether you had taken sufficient care, when you were tortured, and it was torture, with desperate thoughts of what you were to do. In your teens you had the pain, in the middle years the anxiety, later on the sense of overwhelming loss. We were never free; bound by our physiology, condemned, since Eve, to our additional burden.

There was a hold-up at the traffic lights. I reckoned they would have to change three times before I got across. I switched on the radio. Number One on the hit parade begged me to love him tender. Diana would have liked it.

I wondered, with a sob of self-pity, whether Dobbie would be free tomorrow, then, as I crawled forward a few feet, what it must be like to be Ellen Potter; everyone dead. The baby first; enteritis. It probably wouldn't happen today, everyone calling the doctor often, too often, and the new drugs. Six months old; just at the cuddly stage with rounding limbs; watching it sicken and die. Jean and her growth. Cancer was a dirty word in a world where there were few. Trying to find crumbs of comfort to sprinkle on self-inflicted ignorance. You'll be all right, Jeannie. All right! Buried beside the baby. Flesh of your flesh. She hadn't had to bury the boy. They had done it for her, the purveyors of war. One eighteen-year-old please fighting fit. Thank you very much, Mrs Potter, we shall try to return him in good condition. They tried. Five little niggers, now there were two, Ellen and Dad. Listening to the cough, cough, cough, and knowing one more bad winter and that would be that. Did they put him next to Jean and the baby, cosy?

Alone. You tried to make it mean something and failed. Like the war crimes you read about, the tying together of women's legs in child-birth, the bestiality to small children, you attempted a realisation and came up with nothing. The imagination, perhaps fortunately, baulked. You could not suffer vicariously. My own life was more or less untouched by tragedy. My parents were still alive. A second cousin only had failed to return from North Africa, a shadowy youth I scarcely knew in life. The death of grandparents shook for the moment but did not hurt. How must it be to be alone. To have no-one of one's own to talk to. I think I would be desperate if I had to empty the clutter of my mind each day to an unsympathetic wall.

At Hammersmith the traffic was again at a standstill; a girl, alone in the next car, laughed crazily to a funny on the other programme; Dinky cars crossed the fly-over like on Robin's construction set.

Fulham Palace Road she'd said. I asked the policeman on point duty for directions as we crawled by. At this rate I'd be late for dinner. I was unfamiliar with this part of London. People were hurrying now, home from work, one in five coloured. It was difficult to distinguish the names of the roads in the dark. I went right by Wargrave Road and had to turn round. I felt once more a sense of unreality. This morning I hadn't known of the existence of Ellen Potter. All I had been conscious of was Dobbie waiting. It was like some horrid plot, not happening to me. Hawtry Street, Gorringe Place; past a hospital and a cemetery. You forgot how London sprawled with slummy-ended tentacles.

There were few cars now. Ellen Potter had travelled a long way to look at the Christmas shops. Outside the scrap-iron all manner of metal ware was heaped and hung. Round the corner was Colchester Street. I slowed down in an attempt to find number thirteen A. The street was wide, the road littered with peels and rubbish beneath the orange lights.

Mine was the only car. A girl in a thick suit with a tight skirt and slippers with pompons carried home a wrapped loaf, a small boy sat on the kerb picking his nose, empty milk bottles stood on the pavement outside the flat-faced houses with their windows right on the street. I asked a youth in a leather jacket for number thirteen A. He stared at me as if I'd addressed him in Russian. I got out of the car which as if by magic was surrounded by small children, black and white. A green door said number eleven. The next was open, I looked inside, it smelled like a stable, but couldn't see the number.

A woman with her hair in rollers came out.

'Is this number thirteen A?'

'Asright.'

'Does Mrs Potter live here? Ellen Potter.'

'Dunno. I'm upstairs.'

Nobody knew, cared.

There was a door on the right of the stairs. I opened it with Ellen Potter's key. Something tickled my legs as I searched for the light-switch and I almost screamed. The room was lit, the centre of it, at any rate, by a single bulb in a burned shade. Ginger, fur on end, humped his back.

'Pussy, pussy,' I said.

He backed away.

The room was about half the size of Robin's bedroom. My head almost touched the ceiling. Ginger had been lying on the bed, there was a dent in the patchwork quilt.

I looked at the gas-ring with the rusty kettle, the empty grate above which hung a pair of bloomers on a fraying string, the dress and cardigan on the peg behind the door. There was little else to look at. A saucer of milk for Ginger, a bottle of beer almost empty on the table, a shelf with some tea in a packet and a sugar bag, an old fashioned radio with heavy knobs. Could this be all? On the mantelpiece was a photograph in a tarnished frame. A pipe lay in front of it. A plain-faced youth in a paratroopers' beret had scrawled to Mum, love George. Jean was tucked into the corner of the frame a tall young woman with a bicycle. Slit-eyed, Ginger watched me. I laughed at the idea I had had of packing a case with a night-dress, dressing gown, bed-jacket, slippers. I looked under the pillow to make sure but there was nothing. I tried to remember what the old-age pension was, two pounds something, I thought, I didn't really know. The rent for this ghastly place probably took most of that, and a bit of coal, there were signs that there had been a fire. How could people live, not live, exist? The draught came up between the floor boards. There were patches of damp on the walls. I would put the cat out and go. It wasn't right, really not, when someone had given a son. Didn't they get some kind of compensation? Even if they did the money went nowhere today. A few groceries and ten shillings had gone, a pound; like water, slipping away. I could hardly account for it to Tim. It seemed so ridiculous to spend so much on nothing. I went towards Ginger who was dribbling and he dived for the bed. Pussy, pussy, I said, come on, I won't hurt you. A mist hung round the light-bulb. Pussy. Pussy. I grabbed him and he dribbled on to the sleeve of my black coat. I put out the light and shut the door, locking it, and shunted Ginger out into the road.

Fog had hidden the end of Colchester Street. I backed round, trying to avoid the dustbins.

It took me over an hour to get home. By the time I did you could hardly see the bonnet of the car. I got lost twice, finally joined a convoy crawling through the fog, felt exhausted, hysterical. Tim had put on the porch light so that I could see the house.

I had the sensation I'd been away for weeks, the events of the day beginning to tell. Inside the front door everything hit me, the light and the warmth, the thick pile of the grey carpet, the smell of steak pie. It reeked of opulence; fresh flowers even in the Dresden vase on the table. I was filthy from the fog.

'Liz?' Tim called.

'Yes.'

'I was worried. It's come down quite heavily.'

'It took me an hour.' I went in in my coat.

Ellen Potter was sitting in a chair next to Tim's, her hands between her knees. He was mending her watch, trying to, at any rate. He was very good at getting them to pieces but I'd never known him get one back.

'Are you feeling better?' I asked her.

'I am, thank you. I'm sorry you had to go to so much trouble.'

'No trouble at all; it was just a pity about the fog. I put the cat out.'

'I'll get you a drink,' Tim said then looked at the fragments of watch on the arms of the chair, his knees. 'Diana, you do it. Get Mummy a drink.'

She was on the floor with the *Daily Express,* reading the strip on the back page.

'This week!' Tim said.

She heaved herself up. 'What of?'

'Whisky, darling. Just a little.'

She opened the cupboard and Ellen Potter looked at the bottles inside. Gin and whisky, two sorts of sherry, Dubonnet and Cinzano, Vermouth sweet and dry. I thought of the beer bottle in her room.

'Will you excuse me a moment?' she said.

'Have a drink. It will buck you up.'

'I won't, thank you.'

I didn't think we had any beer.

When she'd gone, I said: 'I'm sorry about this.'

'About what?' He was concentrating on

the watch.

'Bringing her here. I couldn't really help it. You should see where she lives.'

'It was very decent of you. Poor old girl. Knocked down, was she?'

'It didn't actually hit her. She just got a fright and fell and bumped her head. It would be kinder if you didn't mess about with that watch.'

'She's upset about it.'

'It would be quicker if she took it in to be repaired.'

'Any idea what it costs to have a watch repaired?'

'I suppose it would be seventeen and six at least.'

Tim raised one eyebrow. 'More like thirty bob.' He understood the situation better than I. I could see now why she'd been anxious.

The whisky warmed me.

Ellen Potter came back. 'I've dished up for you. I thought you'd be tired.'

I stared at her, wondering suddenly if she'd like to stay and be a maid, well more of a housekeeper really, cooking and doing odd jobs. She'd have a comfortable room, warm, plenty to eat...

'Let's eat then,' Tim said. He put the pieces down carefully on the arm of the chair. 'I'm starving.'

Ellen had gone again and Tim put his

arms round me affectionately, holding me close. I thought my God what if I had spent the afternoon with Dobbie.

'Let's go to bed early,' he said kissing me on the mouth.

I looked quickly in Diana's direction as if she understood. She was engrossed still in the newspaper.

'Go and wash and tell Robin it's on the table.'

She stood up.

'And pick up the newspaper.'

Tim slapped my bottom and I went to wash.

Ellen Potter had found plates, everything. I was grateful, felt hungry. By the time you'd cooked it, served it yourself, standing over the heat of the cooker, often you got past eating, especially when you had to jump up in between.

I had the spoon in the pie.

'Dobbie phoned,' Tim said from the top of the table. 'And Jack. They coming round.'

'What did he want?'

'I told you. They'll be round later. They really wanted us to go over there.'

'I meant Dobbie.'

'Nothing particular. He said it wasn't important. I said you'd ring him.'

Not important. Of course that was just to put Tim off. I'd ring him later, arrange something for tomorrow. I couldn't believe the day, *the day,* had come and almost gone and I hadn't after all slept with Dobbie. I looked at Ellen Potter picking at the steak pie, you'd have thought she'd be hungry, and hated her; then I imagined she wasn't there, that I had slept with Dobbie and now I was home, simulating, pretending to be an attentive wife, mother.

'My wife makes fabulous pastry,' Tim said. I winked at Ellen.

'What time are Martha and Jack coming?'

'Nineish.'

I could have done without them tonight especially with Ellen Potter.

'I'm awfully tired.'

'They won't stay late. Jack has a cold. He wants to show me his new camera.'

When we'd finished Diana stayed to help and Ellen said:

'You run along. I'll help your mother.'

'Have you finished your homework?'

'All except some English.'

'Why didn't you do it before instead of reading the newspaper?' I said edgily. 'I wouldn't mind if you read the front page. If I'm not here to chase you... Have you practiced?'

'No. I was just going to.'

'Do get on. It will be ten o'clock again.'

'All the people in my class go to bed at ten.'

'Diana!'

'All right; I'm going.'

'Lovely girl,' Ellen said when she'd gone. 'Love pair.'

'Not bad.'

She watched, fascinated, as I stacked the things in the dishwasher, cutlery in the baskets in the front, plates in the racks on the bottom drawer, jug and glasses on the top. One spoonful of powder, shut the whole thing up.

'Isn't it marvellous!'

Just the saucepans to wash now, they had to be done with Brillo. She took a cloth ready to dry them.

'Do sit down. I'll be finished in five minutes. You've had quite an ordeal.'

'I'm all right again now. I'll be out of your way in the morning.'

I took a deep breath. 'Look, I was wondering if you'd like to stay here for a bit; as a sort of housekeeper ... not doing very much ... but you'd have your room, the one you're in now actually ... and board and lodging...?'

I looked into the washing-up water fishing for the mop.

'You're very kind,' she said drying a saucepan lid. 'But I've got my home...'

Home!

'Not that I'm not used to working. I've always worked. I was with the Co-op for ten years, Clerkenwell way where we lived when my husband was alive. He couldn't work, not the last few years, and there wasn't much by way of a pension. He was in the printing line. Anyway, there's Ginger.'

He must be about a hundred.

'Robin would love to have Ginger. He's had a tortoise and a rabbit at various times...'

'...and there's the cemetery,' she said, 'at the top of the street. It's lovely in the summer, with the roses and sweet-william, watching the people walk through. And the stones are lovely; there's a Boy Scout in uniform, and a violin and bow, he was a bandmaster, and loads of angels, quite big some of them. Such lovely names too, you don't see them today. Clementina, Zenobia, I often wonder what she was like, Violet, Lizzie – "Lizzie Ringwood fell asleep November 27, 1891' – I know them nearly all by heart, you see, Alice, Emily, Ada...'

And Ellen Potter, I thought, looking at the hands twisted with rheumatism, only there was no-one to erect a headstone.

'...of course in the winter it's not so nice but as I said I like walking and watching the children. There's a lot of children in our street. It's not Clerkenwell, of course, we had four rooms there, but of course I don't need it, not on my own. And I've got the radio.'

She made it sound like riches.

'I thought of getting a budgerigar, but I'm afraid with Ginger, for the company, they're chatty little things. Not that I mind being on my own.'

'I should hate it.'

'I did at first. You get used to it. New faces, new surroundings, it takes a while to settle, but I like it up that way and as I say there's the cemetery up the road.'

Seven

The number was engaged. Perhaps he was talking to a woman, Catherine, angry after this afternoon. If I had my time over again I wondered whom I'd marry, Dobbie or Tim? Tim for love, reliability, Dobbie for kicks. It was the kicks one missed. You'd never be sure though with Dobbie, those indolent eyes that brought out the woman in women. You'd be scared to let him out of your sight. Anyway, I loved Tim. Love; an affectionate, devoted attachment, the dictionary said, especially that passionate all-absorbing form of it when the object is one of the opposite sex. Why then did I have my hand on the telephone for Dobbie, envy the names in the gossip columns with the bodies of gods and goddesses and the morals of ferrets, feel I'd missed out knowing it was they who had, on the lasting things, Robin, Diana, Tim? It was still engaged. There was a knock on the door.

'Come in.'

'Who on earth's that downstairs?' Martha said.

I tidied the clothes I had taken off, Dobbie's clothes, and explained about the accident to Ellen Potter.

'Serves you right for rushing away,' Martha said. I remembered that aeons ago I hadn't paid for my lunch.

I hung the dress back in the cupboard. Tomorrow I would wear a different one and perhaps would have better luck. I told Martha that I'd asked Ellen Potter to be our housekeeper.

'What did she say?'

'She said she liked her home. Colchester Street. Martha, you have no idea what it's like, this dreadful place! She hasn't a soul in the world; no money, nothing.'

Martha fingered the gold and ruby dahlia on the lapel of her suit.

'Ask her again. Perhaps you can talk her into it.'

I shut the cupboard. 'She says she's happy.'

'Well then!'

'You know why? Because there's a cemetery at the top of the road where she sits looking at the tombstones. A cemetery.'

'It takes all sorts,' Martha said.

'Martha don't you see? Ellen Potter has nothing, nobody. Look at us.'

Martha was examining her face in the mirror.

'I'm looking.'

'No. I mean look at us. We've got husbands, families, dishwashers, waste-grinders, food-mixers, God knows what...'

'So?' Martha opened her mouth to inspect

her teeth.

'So shouldn't we be the contented ones? Jack's making a mint. If there's anything you want you've only to ask for it, and where do you spend your days? With Dr Raus!'

'My head's going round,' Martha said, 'I had two hours this afternoon and I'm completely exhausted.'

'What's wrong with us? All of us.'

'Darling, if I knew what was wrong with me I wouldn't be paying three guineas a whack to Dr Raus. You're all right, anyway. I always quote you; wonderful wife, mother...'

'If only you knew.'

'Don't tell me you're cracking up, Liz.'

'Not cracking, crumbling. Don't you ever have the feeling that life has done the dirty on you? That it has led you to expect something, then let you down.'

'Darling, do you need Dr Raus.'

'I'm ashamed, in a way. I have so much compared with the Ellen Potters, yet I seem to be worse off.'

'I wouldn't say that.'

'I don't mean materially, although the more you have the more you seem to need, desperately, I mean within. She feels secure, the kind of security that has nothing to do with Life Insurance, I don't. I feel like the blind man in blind man's buff, spinning round and round, trying to reach something.'

'You really do need sorting out.'

'I'll sort myself out. Do you think we're looking in the wrong place?'

'For what?'

'Contentment, peace; I feel so restless. I used to think it would come when we had our own house after that awful furnished flat; then when we had children; then when we could afford someone to help with them; then when we had a terrace to sit on in the summer; then when I had my own car and was independent. There always seems to be something and you know that when you get it everything will be all right, you'll feel this great big sensation of fulfilment. It isn't so. What is it we're after?'

'Dr Raus would know.'

'Has she helped you?'

'It's early days.'

'But Martha you've been going for two years! You can't change your pants without asking her.'

'That's unkind. Besides, it's only the first stage, gradually you get weaned away.'

It reminded me of Farex and Robinson's Groats.

'We've got as far as sex now. We haven't done it, not properly I mean, since Andrew was born. She doesn't mind what you tell her.'

'You could tell me for three guineas a time.'

'You couldn't. That's the whole point.'

'When you think,' I said, 'that there are a hundred Colchester Streets for every Hazelbank.'

'I don't,' Martha said. 'You mustn't.'

The room was tidy.

'Are you coming down?' Martha said.

'You go ahead. I just have a call to make.'

'Who to?'

'No-one you know.'

'You're very secretive today. Who is it? A lover?'

'Of course.'

'What's his name? I won't breathe a word to Tim.'

'Giuseppe.'

'Ask him if he has a friend for me.'

Dobbie's line was still engaged. I called the operator but she verified engaged speaking. I told myself not to panic. A lot of his business was done on the telephone.

Downstairs Martha said, 'Did you know Liz had a lover?'

'Yes, me,' Tim said. 'What will you have to drink?'

'Gin.'

'Jack drank all the gin last night.'

'Whatever you have then. Make it a large one, I feel depressed.'

'That's a change,' Jack said.

'What about?' Tim poured whisky.

'It doesn't have to be *about* anything,'

Martha said. 'You can put the teeniest drain of water in it. If anything, it's about the kitchen floor.'

Ellen Potter was sitting with folded hands in the corner.

'Would you like a drink?' I said and realised it was the third time I had done so that day. She probably thought we were chronic alcoholics.

'I won't, thank you.'

'Are you feeling all right?' Perhaps she'd like to go to bed.

'Oh yes. Fine, thanks.'

'I brought my camera,' Jack said, picking it up from the settee.

'He's like a child with a new toy,' Martha said.

'They always are; with golf clubs and cameras and fishing rods.'

'Smile!' Jack said.

'What now?'

'Yes. Keep still. Put your arm round her, Tim.'

Tim hugged me.

'Thank you.'

'Have you been out?' Martha said. 'You can't see a thing. We had to walk round.'

'It was noble of you to come.'

'Jack wanted to show his toy.'

'Here you are!' Jack said with pride. He held out a photograph.

I took it, Tim and me, Tim smiling.

'That was quick.'

'Good, eh?'

Martha took the photograph. 'You don't look a day older than when you got married. Do they, Jack?'

'Don't feel it,' Tim said. 'Except when I run upstairs.' He patted his tummy. 'It begins to tell.'

'It cost seventy-five pounds wholesale,' Jack said. 'Chap I know imports them.'

I looked quickly at Ellen Potter.

'Pretty good I think. By the time you've had the old-fashioned kind developed and printed you've lost interest.'

'You don't get the same definition,' Tim said.

Jack examined the photograph. 'There's nothing wrong with that.'

'It's not bad.'

'It's bloody good.'

'You can't compare it to my Voigtländer.'

'You can you know.'

'It's all right for an amateur!'

'Stop it you two!' Martha said. 'Have you thought about next summer? We thought we'd try Spain.'

'You don't like the heat.'

'There's a little place in the North, the Spaniards go there, it's not so hot and supposed to be absolutely divine. Why don't you come?'

'Tim won't. Not to Spain. All those people

284

languishing in jails and being tortured. He won't spend money in a fascist country.'

'Tim needs a halo. You can't worry about all these little things. We're planning a holiday not a political meeting.'

It was pointless to pursue the matter.

'We're thinking of taking the car,' Martha said.

'You don't like driving though.'

'I don't like planes, ships, or trains, either. I don't want to stay at home.'

'You need a magic carpet,' Tim said.

'I need something.'

'A good spank!' Jack said.

'Dr Raus would be horrified. It would solve nothing. Like spanking a child.'

'Rubbish! I had a few in my day.'

'Where has it got you?'

'At least I can stand on my own feet.'

'That's not fair,' Martha said beginning to snivel.

'Look, why don't you girls make some coffee?' Tim said.

'I think I'll go home,' Martha said.

'You can't, darling. It's foggy. You'd get lost. I'd have to send Dr Raus for you.'

'That's enough!'

'I'm only teasing,' Jack said and went to sit next to Tim. 'Have you a piece of paper? I'll write something down for you. Ring your broker first thing in the morning.'

Jack always had good tips. The trouble was

that with the ones he passed on to Tim something always went wrong. From the horse's mouth, he said, utterly hush-hush from someone on the board. We ended up with a scrap of paper every time he came. Nine out of ten Tim threw away. Ironically they'd prosper. The one he'd do something about would inevitably go astray.

'I've had enough of your tips,' Tim said.

'You'll be sorry.' Jack flicked his moustache. 'You've your children to think of. This is right from the top.'

'So was Cleveland United?'

'That was unfortunate.'

'And that Coventry firm. Bricks.'

'Shoes. I'm only trying to help you.'

'I know. Tell me what it is and I'll see if I care for the sound.'

'They're only ten and threepence,' Jack said. 'Buy a thousand in the morning. You'll be grateful to me for this.'

They had forgotten about Ellen Potter. She was taking it all in. I felt slightly ashamed. Thousands when I doubted if she had ten.

'We're going to make some coffee,' I said not wanting to leave her while Tim and Jack were talking in telephone numbers. 'Would you like to come?'

In the kitchen she said: 'I won't have any coffee, if you don't mind. It keeps me awake.'

'Me too,' Martha said. 'Sometimes I can't

resist. I adore coffee and it just finishes me. I have to get up and take a pill but by that time I'm usually too far gone and just toss and turn till morning.'

'Would you mind if I went to bed?' Ellen said.

'Of course not. Would you like me to bring you some warm milk?'

'No nothing at all, thanks. I enjoyed my supper, it was ever so nice. There is one thing.'

'Yes?'

'Could I have a glass for my teeth?'

Upstairs I gave her a towel and showed her where everything was. I wasn't sure whether I should offer a night-dress and thought because there had been no signs of one in Colchester Street, perhaps not. Martha disagreed. 'Don't be silly, darling, she's a woman. Of course she'd like one even if she hasn't got one at home. A hot bath too with lashings of Lentheric or whatever it is you use.'

I ran the bath and Ellen Potter stood in the doorway clutching the nylon nightie.

'It'll be lovely having a hot bath,' she said, 'I shan't want to come out.'

I told her not to lock the door and went down.

'You were right,' I told Martha. 'About the bath.'

'I know I was. Because she doesn't have all

these things doesn't mean to say she can't appreciate them.'

'Why doesn't she want to stay here then?'

'Independent, I suppose. At least she's her own boss.'

'I keep thinking of that ghastly room she lives in.'

'I wouldn't worry about it. It doesn't appear to worry her.'

'We get wild,' I said, 'if we have to stay one night in a hotel without a private bathroom.'

'I can't bear it,' Martha said, 'I'd walk out.'

I left Martha to get the tray ready for the coffee and went upstairs to ring Dobbie.

It rang this time. Dobbie, I got ready to say, Dobbie. It rang and rang the hollow tone you get when it rings in an empty flat. I sat on the bed holding the receiver to my ear listening to the sound, no-one wanting me; Martha downstairs busy with herself and Dr Raus, Tim and Jack content with each other in the sitting-room, a strange person for whom I felt nothing at all in my bath.

Dobbie had probably gone out in the fog for dinner. He wasn't one of the handy bachelor cook types who could knock up a steak *au poivre* in the twinkling of an eye and used his kitchen only for breakfast. I didn't want to go downstairs again, to be sociable with Martha and Jack. I was tired, would have liked to crawl into bed pulling the covers – I had a sudden image of Ellen Potter's patchwork quilt – up over my head. My day wasn't finished though. Tim had indicated he wanted to make love. I wished I was anywhere, Japan, Morocco, a South Sea Island; anywhere where there was colour, not the rose-and-gold of the bedroom silted with fog, I'd thought it was chic when it was done, now everyone had rose and gold and I'd gone over to the elegance of white, but the reds and greens and blues of the tropics beneath a blazing sun. I'd be walking on palm-fringed shores, golden-limbed, wearing, with grace, a sarong. A gardenia would hold back my long hair, warm sands embrace my naked feet...

'Kettle's boiling,' Martha called up the stairs. 'Shall I use the grey pot?'

Eight

We held the front door open while they made their way down the drive. When we shut it a belch of fog came into the house.

'Filthy night,' Tim said. 'I hope it clears by the morning.'

'Doesn't look as if it's going to. It's absolutely yellow. I wish we lived in the South of France.'

'You'd be moaning about the mosquitoes if we did. Remember that year in Juan les Pins?'

'They seem to like me. It's not my fault.'

'I didn't say it was. I was just pointing out that nothing is quite what it seems. There are disadvantages associated with everything.'

'I think I'd prefer mosquitoes to fog.'

'The trouble with you, Liz, is that you're never satisfied.'

I stopped, a full ashtray from Jack's cigar in my hand.

'That's not true!'

'It is you know. You're always wishing you were somewhere else doing something different.'

It was true.

'Why don't you just accept things?'

I picked up a piece of paper from the table. 'Do you want this?'

'It's Jack's tip.'

'Going to do anything about it?'

'No. Throw it away.'

Tim followed me into the kitchen with the dirty glasses. 'Why don't you try to be a bit more realistic?'

'In what way?'

'Face the facts. Don't keep thinking that you could have done better.'

'I don't really.'

'*I'm* perfectly happy.'

'It's just different with men. They're less complicated.'

'Just as well. I don't think I could exist if I had your worries.'

Back in the sitting-room Tim picked up the coffee tray. I took the photograph Jack had taken of Tim and me off the bookcase.

'Rotten photograph,' Tim said.

'It's not bad.'

'No definition at all. It's not sharp.'

'Looks all right to me. I don't know why you make such a fuss.'

'The same reason as you make a fuss over curtains and things. I happen to be interested.'

He put the tray down in the kitchen and put his arms round me.

'Getting on each other's nerves a bit aren't we?'

'It must be the fog.' It was the day. The strain of going to spend the afternoon with Dobbie and not going. The acquiring of Ellen Potter.

'You must have had quite a day with the old lady.'

'Yes.'

'Come to bed then. I'll cheer you up.'

'I must clear away first.'

Tim released me and sighed knowing I was being perverse. I could quite well have left the rest of the fiddling about until morning.'

'I haven't laid the breakfast yet.'

'Okay. You don't mind if I go up?'

'No.'

'How long will you be?' the look in his eyes was familiar.

I looked away. 'Not long.'

'Have you seen my book?'

'It's by the bed.'

It was very quiet when he'd gone, the day, at midnight, almost over. Almost. I put the cups into the dishwasher, upside down on the top shelf. I have spent the afternoon with my lover, I told myself, upstairs my husband is waiting to make love with me. As far as desire goes I am an empty shell. What do I do? He'd never guess of course, Tim I mean, I could say I was tired, had a head-ache, toothache, he'd be all sympathy. Suddenly my life seemed to have got into a

292

tangle. I hated my nice kitchen with its willing, chromium-trimmed servants. It was clinical, soulless. Practical it was true. I was not in a practical mood. What mood was I in? Tim was right, he was so often, I was never satisfied. Always the grass somewhere else seemed greener; it was a thing you had to live with learning to tell yourself it wasn't. It was though, you knew it was. A teaspoon slipped through the little basket into the works of the dishwasher. I had put it in the wrong way round, not paying attention, thinking of someone else. It meant removing the bottom tray to get it out. I'd better do it. In the morning I'd forget and the whole thing was liable to jam.

I'd just replaced the tray, it was quite heavy, when Tim called, 'Liz!'

'Yes.'

'What on earth are you doing?'

'Dropped a teaspoon in the dishwasher. I shan't be long.'

Breakfast for another day. When I'd finished it looked pleasing. Robin's dirty shoes spoiled the kitchen. I'd forgotten to do them. They'd have to wait until the morning when I'd be even less inclined. He was supposed to clean them himself but he managed to get black polish on to the floor, his shirt, hands, then grabbed the banisters on the way up to wash. It was easier to do them for him. At least he knew when they

293

were dirty. Diana never bothered. Just the tray to put away in the special tray space between two of the cupboards. There was a satisfaction in having a place for everything, a cleanness, a completeness even if it was clinical. That was the kitchen done.

In the sitting-room I straightened things, the coffee table Jack had pulled forward to write his tip on, the chair where Ellen Potter had sat by the window, the cigarette box which looked best at a certain angle. The Limoges ashtray that Mrs Mac had broken in the morning was on the mantelpiece. Surely she hadn't repaired it, she'd never repaired anything yet, besides I'd told her Tim would do it.

I picked it up. One half only came into my hand the other like a bombed house stood sheered away. I put it back, carefully arranged, as if it was in one piece.

I looked at the curtains. Martha always opened hers at night so that when she came down in the morning it was light instead of dark. I didn't like the idea. Tim came down first anyway and opened them.

Just the lights. The sitting-room, kitchen hall, leaving the one on the stairs which you could switch from up or down.

The carpet on the stairs was beginning to show wear on the edges of the treads. I would have to get it moved before it went any further. Carpet was so frightfully expensive; everything really. A hundred pounds today went nowhere on furniture if you didn't want to buy absolute rubbish. Of course it was the tax and everyone wanting more wages and as soon as the increases were granted it was time for the next one. So it went on. If it wasn't strikes it was the threat of wars in various places with the nasty thought that we all might soon be involved and masses of spies everywhere suddenly getting caught and everything in a thoroughly nasty state. Perhaps it had never been any better, I don't know, only that suddenly there seemed so much to worry about, everything uncertain in the world and at home. Such a strain. You never knew if anything was going to be all right.

'Liz,' Tim said when I was on the landing.

'Who did you think it was?'

'You're taking an age.'

'Shh. You'll wake Mrs Potter.'

'I'd forgotten about her.'

I opened the door of Diana's bedroom. I always looked in on them before I went to bed, a habit which had died hard from their babyhood. She hadn't opened her window or folded her bed cover. Her school clothes were in a heap on the armchair topped by the white spider of her suspender belt. There were glass animals in a case and a copy of *Woman and Beauty* on the bed. She'd probably been reading for hours. The bedclothes and eiderdown were slopping on to the floor, the pillow halfway down the bed. I didn't straighten her up. She was a light sleeper and would only toss herself into a mess again anyway. She liked it, she said, it was comfortable.

In Robin's room everything was neat, even the way he lay, the bed tucked in as it had been when he got into it. He slept like a top and nothing I'd do would waken him. There was nothing to do. The window was open, his clothes tidy, clean ones ready for the morning, his comic neatly folded on the table beside the bed.

I loved them when they slept. A surge of maternal feeling emanated from me into the semi-dark. It was a moment when I felt they were my flesh and blood and that I had shaped them. By day at loggerheads, chiefly with Diana, I wondered where they had been spawned.

In the spare bedroom Ellen Potter scarcely made a bump in the bed and might for all I knew be dead. The thought frightened me and I crept towards her to listen for breathing. It was very gentle like a child's. The other end of the see-saw. Robin and Diana slept the sleep of anticipation, Ellen Potter of realisation; if there was disillusionment she hadn't seemed to notice. I, I suppose, was balanced in the middle. I wondered whether I would come down with a bump.

'Come on,' Tim said, leaning against the rose-spattered pillows which always made me want to laugh. 'This book's tedious as hell. Did you phone about the cooker?'

'The cooker?'

'Wake up. About the chip. You said this morning you would get on to the electricity company.'

This morning. A hundred light years away.

'I haven't had time.'

'No time! I don't know what you do with yourself all day.'

It was just as well.

'I hope the children are quiet in the morning,' I said. 'It would be a pity to wake the old girl.'

'She'll be up at six,' Tim said. 'Old people always are. When you can sleep you don't want to.'

I yawned at myself in the mirror. 'I could sleep for a week.'

'That's how it is.'

'It's unfair.'

'Life is full of paradoxes.'

'I wonder which one of us will die first.'

'Why, suddenly?'

'Ellen Potter. Old people always make me morbid. They have that "on the way out" look. Robin asked me yesterday if we were both killed in a motor accident where he would find the money.'

'What did you tell him.'

'On the mantelpiece. He likes to be prepared. I think it will be me.'

'Or me. It's no use worrying.'

'I'm not worried. I just wondered. It would be nice if you knew. Could look into the future.'

'You probably wouldn't like it one bit.'

'Probably. Throw my nightie.'

It landed on the floor.

'Sorry.'

'I could do with a new roll-on. As soon as you find one you like they stop making it and produce something else.

'That's business. Turn round. You're prettier than all those girls in Italy.'

'Too much here and not enough here.'

'Hurry and come to bed.'

'Diana's been at the cleansing cream. She's incapable of putting the lid back.'

'Why don't you leave the girl alone?'

'I try to. She makes me so mad. Have you noticed she's blossoming in all directions?'

'She'll be keeping me out of the bathroom soon.'

'It alters one's status.'

'How?'

'Mother of a teenage daughter. Different to having young children. Matronly.'

'There's nothing matronly about you.'

'Sometimes I feel it. I hear myself talking and sound exactly like my mother.'

'Stop kicking against it. I'll be forty next

birthday. That's something.'

'Couldn't you stay thirty-nine?'

'Or twenty-seven, like Martha?'

'She looks years older than me.'

'Don't sound so pleased about it.'

'Well she does. It's because she's so fat. She carries on ad nauseam with this dieting business and never stops eating.'

'I don't suppose Jack objects.'

'I don't think he gets the chance.'

'How do you mean?'

'He never gets close enough.'

'You girls. Talk about nothing but sex.'

'Dr Raus is trying to cure her.'

'I could cure her. I bet Jack goes about it like a bull in a china shop.'

'What a curious simile!'

'Apt though. Don't be long in there.'

I loved my bathroom, sea green tiles and black fish swimming across the curtains. In our first flat there had been what we called a wash-box with a strip of lino beside the bath barely large enough to stand on. For Ellen Potter not even that.

The water rushed greenly into the basin for my stockings. I had to keep Diana in nylons now; weekends at any rate. She'd only have them on a few hours and there'd be a wail of Mummy, well it wasn't my fault... It was futile to say in my day we didn't wear nylons there weren't such things anyway and we stayed in black wool for school until eighteen. Sometimes I'd wait outside the school for Diana watching the stockings, usually laddered, and the bouffant hair-dos that looked as if they needed a good brush and feel about a hundred. There had been a revolution. Not a civil nor a bloody one. I had been caught in it. I tried to understand.

I hung the stockings over the towel taking care they didn't touch the hot pipes, ran the cold water for my teeth. The children had better teeth than mine which were full of fillings. They liked the toothpaste with the stripe in it, it was a good gimmick. They didn't mind going to the dentist either, that too had changed. We used to go in fear and trembling. I still did needing one of the pills from the brown bottle and an injection before anything was done. Robin and Diana nipped upstairs with the nurse as if they were going to the cinema and came down talking about the next job on hand. They'd done it since babies, credit I suppose due to the dentist, the new psychology.

I took the nourishing cream out and put it back in the mirrored cupboard, it wasn't pleasant to kiss. I brushed my hair back from my face, thinking I looked young at night, relaxed, unless it was the soft lights in the bathroom, the flattering neckline of my dressing gown.

The hand cream was green matching the

tiles. Small things like that gave pleasure, Diana had been at it, the top was sticky.

'Liz!'

'Coming.'

Tim had put down his book and was lying with his arms behind his head watching me.

I turned off the radiator and opened the window automatically then shut it again quickly.

'You let the fog in.'

'I forgot. I hate sleeping with the window shut.'

'It's better than breathing in all that muck.'

The bedside clock showed 12.20. I got into bed beside Tim.

'Blast!' I said.

'What's wrong?'

'I've forgotten something.'

He put his arms round me pulling me into his side of the bed which was warm. 'Don't worry I'll get it later.'

'How much later?'

'Much, much later.'

'We have to get up in the morning. I don't know why Martha and Jack stay so late. They never go to bed before one.'

'Don't let's talk about Martha and Jack.'

Tim took off the nightdress I'd only just put on. I looked at the ceiling, zephyr, just a trace of pink echoing the rose of the carpet. I wouldn't ring Dobbie, not in the morning, any time, it wasn't going to solve anything.

'Liz. Honey. Liz.'

I thought that tomorrow we might have veal for a change. Martha had given me a recipe with red peppers.

The publishers hope that this book has given you enjoyable reading. Large Print Books are especially designed to be as easy to see and hold as possible. If you wish a complete list of our books please ask at your local library or write directly to:

Dales Large Print Books
Magna House, Long Preston,
Skipton, North Yorkshire.
BD23 4ND